READ IN THE HAY
Issue n° 13 — Summer 2019

PART 1

On the cover, film star OWEN WILSON, and in the garden by Milan Zrnic.

PART 2

The Book of the Season is MEDITATIONS by Marcus Aurelius, handwritten in Koine Greek in the second century AD and first appearing in print in 1559.

Pattern inspired by Friedrich Hottenroth's 1896 encyclopaedia *The Art of Costumes: Ancient and Modern Peoples' Costumes, Weapons, Jewels, Ceramics, Utensils, Tools, Furniture, Etc.*

A surrealist poster from the
1970s by German designer
GUNTER RAMBOW.

HOLD ME

In March of this year, the *New York Post* ran a story with the headline 'Bella and Gigi Hadid make books the hot new accessory of 2019'. The American sisters, who are both ludicrously famous models, had been spotted in separate situations in Milan and Paris, each carrying a book in a somewhat ostentatious fashion. Bella gripped a hardback of Stephen King's new novel, *The Outsider*. Gigi was holding a paperback of Albert Camus' *The Stranger*. The accompanying story pointed out how well the books matched the models' outfits.

This and the headline were widely derided, mostly for their implication that the Hadids were more interested in being seen with the books than they were in reading them. An unkind allegation, but these days a typical one. The existence of technology that encourages us to frack our lives, our thoughts and our surroundings in return for micro-applause has created a tendency to view everything through this prism, to suspect that nothing is done on its own terms, that everything is for appearance.

Incidentally the original French title of Camus' existentialist classic, *L'Étranger*, is not always translated as *The Stranger* but sometimes as *The Outsider*, the exact same title as King's book. This can't be a coincidence, surely? It must have been coordinated — the Hadids holding the books, the books discreetly pointing at one another. But why? The signs are that this didn't belong to some lightweight tradition of culture-signalling but the thrilling world of the literary riddle. If celebrities want to become walking cryptic crosswords, this should probably be encouraged. If *The Happy Reader* ever finds out the solution, you will read about it in the Snippets.

THE HAPPY READER
Bookish Magazine
Issue nº 13 — Summer 2019

The Happy Reader is
a collaboration between
Penguin Books and
Fantastic Man

EDITOR-IN-CHIEF
Seb Emina

MANAGING EDITOR
Maria Bedford

ART DIRECTOR
Tom Etherington

EDITORIAL DIRECTORS
Jop van Bennekom
Gert Jonkers

PICTURE RESEARCH
Frances Roper

PRODUCTION
Ilaria Rovera

DESIGN CONCEPT
Jop van Bennekom
Helios Capdevila

BRAND DIRECTOR
Sam Voulters

PUBLISHER
Stefan McGrath

CONTRIBUTORS
Geoff Dyer, Amanda Fortini,
Jordan Kelly, Jocelyn Lee,
Deborah Levy, Harriet
Alida Lye, Jamie MacRae,
Martin Parr, Lex Paulson,
Massimo Pigliucci, Gunter
Rambow, Simen Røyseland,
Sadie Stein, Milan Zrnic.

THANK YOU
Magnus Åkesson, Helen
Conford, Lauren Elkin, Linda
Fallon, Camille Ferté, Eliot
Haworth, Ivan Hibbert, Matthew
Hutchinson, Rebecca Lee, Penny
Martin, Yelena Moskovich, Liz
Parsons, Caroline Pretty, Nadja
Spiegelman, Antonia Webb.

Penguin Books
80 Strand
London WC2R 0RL

info@thehappyreader.com
www.thehappyreader.com

SNIPPETS

A summery salad of news and information, inspiration and opportunities.

BURN BEFORE READING — A graphic design studio has published a heat-sensitive edition of Ray Bradbury's novel *Fahrenheit 451*. The book, of which just 100 copies have been printed, is by Super Terrain, a studio in Nantes, France, and costs $451 per copy. Its pages are completely black until exposed to an open flame or other heat-emanating item such as a car engine or hot mouth.

INTERN — Former Taiwanese president Ma-Ying Jeou left office in a fog of unpopularity in 2016 but has lately been trying to rehabilitate his image. For example, he has looked to demonstrate his man-of-the-people credentials by working in a Taipei bookshop, for a day.

TATTOO SUMMIT — The city of Chattanooga, Tennessee, hosted a conference dedicated to literary tattoos, especially, to be honest, those inspired by Harry Potter.

TREASURE — British artist Jeremy Deller appeared on BBC radio programme *Desert Island Discs*, in which guests reveal which records they'd ideally want to have with them if stranded on a desert island. Each guest chooses a book as well, and Deller opted for the evocative sentimental power of otherwise useless maps: the *London A–Z Street Atlas*.

ERA OVER — The death of Karl Lagerfeld was sad news for the fashion industry but also for Paris bookselling. The designer was a voracious reader whose personal library was said to contain more than 300,000 titles and whose tastes ranged from the poetry of Emily Dickinson to the aesthetic theorising of George Santayana. One of his favourite bookshops was Galignani, the chic bilingual outlet on rue de Rivoli in Paris, just across the Seine from Lagerfeld's own boutique bookstore, 7L.

SOCIAL JUSTICE — The website Wattpad, a wildly popular forum for sharing rough-and-ready fiction with like-minded authors, is launching a publishing division in the autumn. Wattpad Books will create printed versions of works by its most popular users. First titles include *Trapeze* by Leigh Ansell, about a trapeze artist whose career is thwarted by a tragic accident, and V. S. Santoni's school drama *I'm a Gay Wizard.*

COMIC BOOKER — Each year the French city of Angoulême hosts what is arguably the world's most important festival of international comic books. For the first time, this year's instalment saw both of the festival's most important awards go to female authors. The Fauve d'Or, or Golden Wildcat, for the year's best release, was given to *My Favorite Thing is Monsters*, the debut graphic novel by Emil Ferris, while the Grand Prix, Angoulême's prestigious lifetime achievement award, was taken by manga artist Rumiko Takahashi.

TOLSTOY — Unorthodox pop star Grimes, a former cover star for this magazine, put off finishing her new album and took to working on a fantasy novel instead. 'It centres around a lesbian romance,' the Canadian artist announced online, 'between a demon named War and an angel named Peace.'

SUMMER JOB — Monk's House, the former country retreat of Virginia Woolf and her husband Leonard, is looking for volunteers. The residence, which Woolf described as 'a house of many doors', brings a constant stream of pilgrims to its address in the middle of the East Sussex countryside.

CHEEK — Men's magazine *Penthouse*, publisher of lifestyle content and soft porn since the 1960s, has hired a new book critic in the form of reality TV star Farrah Abraham. Launching her quest to assess how both classic and contemporary titles might connect with regular American women, Abraham's first column looks at Joan Didion's *Slouching Towards Bethlehem* (1968) and is headlined: 'Joan Didion is a Gin-Drinking Bore Who Writes Convoluted Books'. In the end, Abraham's verdict is the same as that of many book critics, only more openly stated: 'If you want a book that that discusses real issues, you are better off picking up my memoir.'

BOOKLANDS — If 'most readerly nation' is awarded according to the time spent reading by an average adult, then 2018's most readerly nations were, respectively, India, Thailand and China.

OWEN WILSON

In conversation with
AMANDA FORTINI

Portraits by
MILAN ZRNIC

Owen Wilson, the movie star, loves to read. His mind is filled with quotes from favourite books, which he is able to recall at a moment's notice. They have helped him a lot in becoming the funniest actor of his generation, with films such as *The Royal Tenenbaums*, *Midnight in Paris* and *Zoolander* showcasing a weird knack for introducing references and catch phrases to our global lexicon. The amazing thing is, he never even seems to be trying. In this rare interview, Wilson, 50, invites *The Happy Reader* to get to know him while perusing the classic and not-so-classic titles stacked up around his home.

SANTA MONICA

Owen Wilson lives in Santa Monica, California, in a quiet, green residential neighbourhood that, on the early spring day we meet, smells overwhelmingly like flowers. We want to do the interview surrounded by books: there are some in the alcove front sitting room, and an entire wall of them in his bedroom, so we head upstairs. The room is a light, cosy space, with lots of framed art, a pale Moroccan rug, and a large television embedded in the wall of books.

Wilson, who is wearing jeans and a grey button-down shirt, is in sock feet and has a Grateful Dead baseball cap perched on his head. He grew up in an upper-middle-class family in Dallas, Texas: his mother, Laura, is a photographer who worked for Richard Avedon; his father, Robert, ran an ad agency and wrote and edited books in his spare time. Wilson was the middle of three boys: his brothers, Andrew and Luke, both actors, are regulars in the comic universe Wilson created with Wes Anderson, whom he met when they were undergraduates at the University of Texas at Austin. The trilogy of independent films they wrote together — *Bottle Rocket, Rushmore and Royal Tenenbaums* — are considered modern classics, some of the funniest, quirkiest, kookiest, most delightful movies of the mid to late 1990s and early 2000s.

In other comedies, like the blockbusters *Wedding Crashers* and *Zoolander*, Wilson solidified his distinct comic persona — an apparently guileless, slightly dazed surfer-type who actually has a slyness and a kind of twinkly amusement running just beneath his placid surface — and gained a reputation for contributing his own hilarious lines. Even in more serious roles, like the aspiring writer he plays in Woody Allen's *Midnight in Paris*, his essential Owen Wilson-ness glints through. In person, he talks slowly, with a syrupy south-western drawl — his voice is like chewing gum being pulled — and a not very careful listener might miss how smart and perceptive he is. He has just returned from a trip to Panama and Cuba, and will soon leave for Maui, where he's owned a house for the past twelve years. He pulls up a chair for me, and we sit in front of the bookshelves to talk. I quickly realise that his comedic genius, a mix of odd intonation, precise references and impeccable timing, will be difficult to convey in print.

One of his infamous, deceptively artless 'Wows' or, in this interview, a well-placed, drawn-out 'Yeah' contains a world of humour.

AMANDA: What were you doing in Cuba and Panama? Was it just a vacation?

OWEN: Just a trip. Somebody having a birthday in Havana organised this kind of conference. You know, they had a chef from a good Cuban restaurant, and you'd go meet Cuban entrepreneurs. So I was there for a couple days and then continued on to Panama City, where I have some friends.

A: Did you go see Hemingway's house in Cuba, Finca Vigía?

O: No. I got there Saturday. It was closed on Sunday. And then, Monday, when I left, it wasn't open in time. I really wanted to see that, but I think I'll be back. Do you read much Hemingway?

A: I've read a lot, but I haven't read any recently. What about you? Your character in *Midnight in Paris* encounters Hemingway a couple of times.

O: I've read the ones you read in school, like *The Old Man and the Sea* and *A Farewell to Arms,* and then I'll quote him sometimes. You know that quote from *A Moveable Feast* about loving Paris: 'If you are lucky enough to have lived in Paris as a young man, then wherever you go the rest of your life, it stays with you, for Paris —'

A: '— is a moveable feast.'

O: It's pretty good. And then I like that one from — what's the one that they made into a movie with Gary Cooper? — *A Farewell to Arms.* That's the one with that great quote that the world breaks everyone. And many are strong in the broken places.

A: I love *A Farewell to Arms.* It's the one that I've read multiple times, and it's genuinely affecting, I think. Of course it's kind of out of fashion to like Hemingway.

O: It is. He gets swallowed up with the macho cliché. That can kind of happen. Like Elvis, I feel, can sometimes get co-opted by the jumpsuits and the Las Vegas.

A: The late, fat Elvis. The 'Suspicious Minds' Elvis.

O: But you forget the radical Elvis. Then you hear a song like those first recordings of 'Blue Moon' that are incredible — so haunting.

A: Once I was on a long drive, from Montana to LA, and there was a late-night radio show about Elvis on, playing old Elvis songs, and

Wilson has been known to kick a ball around with Hollywood United, the soccer team founded by The Sex Pistols' Steve Jones.

I listened to it for like three hours, and suddenly I understood what you're talking about. I never 'got' Elvis before that. He is amazing.

O: I had the same thing. My brother was reading those Guralnick biographies on Elvis that were really good, *Last Train to Memphis* and *Careless Love*. I started reading those and they really shifted me on to him, and just made me appreciate him so much and really love him.

A: Which brother was that?

O: Luke. Luke's big on biographies, especially rock-and-roll biographies and Dylan biographies.

A: Did you read Dylan's autobiography?

O: *Chronicles*. Yeah, I did that. I didn't love it as much as everybody did. It was a little bit... the way it's written doesn't sound like — when you read Johnny Cash, writing in his voice, it sounds like his voice. Dylan sometimes, I feel, kind of adopts voices.

A: I saw a Richard Ford novel there, on the ottoman — which was that, by the way?

O: *The Sportswriter*. That's definitely one of my favourites.

A: Do you like to read fiction?

O: I tend to read a lot more biographies and history. Right now I'm reading Wilfred Thesiger, who was an English explorer and wrote this book, *Arabian Sands*, that my mother gave me after we went to Dubai, and it just lay on my shelf for years. It was only recently, when I went to Egypt, that I came across it, and was like, 'OK, let me bring this,' and started reading it and just loved it. It's an account of his time travelling with the Bedouin and across the Empty Quarter of the Arabian Desert.

A: When did you go to Dubai with your mom?

O: Maybe like eight years ago.

A: Did your parents read a lot when you were growing up?

O: Yeah. I mean, we would accuse my dad of always having a lot of books that he didn't finish. This Library of America series, right here, that was in Dallas, but then came out here, Luke used to call it the 'Most Unread Series of Books'. My dad loved these but I don't know if he ever really read them. This is my dad [he points to a black-and-white framed headshot on the shelf behind us].

A: I read that he was a TV executive. Is that right?

O: No, he was the right-hand man for this kind of heavy-hitter in

1. GURALNICK
—
As far as twentieth-century music biographies go, Peter Guralnick, 75, is a Big Name. His latest book, *Sam Phillips: The Man Who Invented Rock 'n' Roll*, about the producer credited with discovering Elvis and Johnny Cash, is being developed into a movie starring Leonardo DiCaprio.

2. THE SNOW LEOPARD
—
Peter Matthiessen's travel classic details a trip to Nepal in search of an elusive wildcat. Matthiessen lived in Paris in the early 1950s and was a co-founder of literary magazine *The Paris Review*, which he later said he invented as cover for his other job as a CIA agent.

Dallas, Ralph Rogers, who made my dad the head of the PBS station; he was twenty-eight at the time. My dad did that for a while, and then he started an ad agency. My dad had an appreciation for language, and even used to write a column in *D Magazine*, and sometimes would submit something to the local newspaper. He did a few books also.

A: If you could characterise your childhood, just in general, what was it like?

O: I think it was a pretty good childhood. Just, you know, growing up in the seventies — a much looser time than now. I think that's maybe a better way, although I'm sure people don't want to go back to a time where kids rode bikes without helmets and no sunscreen and would come back just fried as a lobster and everyone would say how 'healthy' you looked. But that's the way I grew up, where you were a little bit on your own, in terms of being able to go out with your friends and being able to ride your bike up to 7-Eleven and play *Asteroids*, or just cruise around and look for mischief and adventure.

A: That's very similar to my childhood, actually. Were you close to your dad?

O: I really idolised my dad. I read a book, last year, that meant a lot to me, *The Snow Leopard*. My dad passed away a couple of years ago but I have some of his — he would write, and collect newspaper articles that he was interested in, and I came across a note that he had written to me, quoting something from *The Snow Leopard*. And, of course, you get notes from your parents and 'Oh, OK' and they don't really register that much. And so it was funny to come across that letter.

A: Wait, you were already reading the book?

O: I was reading it when I came across it.

A: How crazy.

O: At this point the book was already having a big impact on me, so it was a funny connection with him, that he had read the book and appreciated it and quoted something from it to me.

A: Do you remember what he quoted?

O: It was about how the monks would carry a dagger to cut through delusions. And he was writing that note to me at a time when I was struggling with, uh — I'd had some issues with drugs in my late twenties.

A: Well, that's so amazing. I thought you were going to say that you picked up *The Snow Leopard* because your dad recommended it, but it was a serendipitous thing that you were already reading it when you found it. Kind of gives you chills. Goosebumps.

O: Exactly.

A: I occasionally find these letters with little newspaper clippings from my grandparents that they would send me when I was in my twenties and I just kind of ignored. I feel so guilty about it now. But, you know, kids.

O: You just hope it clicks in later. Now, having two boys, you notice stuff go in one ear and out the other. That's just the nature of the roles we get cast in. Now I'm cast in the role of the dad.

A: How old are they, your boys?

O: Eight and five. It's funny, I've been reading stories to them, but I just read a book that's the first one I've read to them where it's like, OK, this is a *good book* that I was into also.

A: What was it?

O: It's called *Ghost* by Jason Reynolds. It was a finalist for a National Book Award. I have it there [he turns and points to the shelf]. It's a really good story. Well, I went and got all of them — now there's a whole series of them — but this was the book. I actually reached out to him.

A: Do you read to your sons a lot?

O: Every night. I got read to a lot — not just my parents but my grandmother, even after I could read and was reading books on my own, they would still get a book and read to me.

A: Did your grandma live with you?

O: No, she lived in Marshfield, Massachusetts, and I grew up in Dallas, but in the summers I would go up to visit her and there was also a bookmobile. Did you ever hear of bookmobiles?

A: I did! [laughs]

O: I would go visit her and we'd go to the bookmobile. I feel like reading made such a difference in my life. In fact, I think not having really — I was an English major, but I didn't graduate and, you know, I didn't really read all that much in college, but as a little kid I read a *ton*. Childhood was probably my heyday as a reader. I loved Louis L'Amour. I read a ton of Louis L'Amour books as a kid.

A: He wrote tons.

3. MATT CHRISTOPHER
—
Until his death in 1997, the children's author wrote more than one hundred novels, mostly about sports. His family then registered his name as a trademark, allowing him to publish (with the help of various ghostwriters) a further eighty books from beyond the grave.

4. MILITARY SCHOOL
—
Wilson was sent to New Mexico Military School in Roswell, New Mexico after being expelled from St Mark's school in Dallas. 'I got expelled for cheating in geometry,' he tells *The Happy Reader*. 'I was handing in these extra credit problems with 50 lines of theorems and proofs because we had gotten the teacher's edition of the book that had those answers... It wasn't hard to catch me.'

O: Tons. My mom worked for Avedon for ten years in the American West and he liked Louis L'Amour so he'd send me boxes of them.

A: What is your mom doing now?

O: She's doing a photography book on writers, and I think she's actually in Europe right now shooting the South African writer Coetzee, who did that book *Disgrace*. That's a great book. Oh God. She's gotten a lot of great authors. It's been years that she's been doing it, but she got Carlos Fuentes and I think Gabriel García Márquez. Who is the Minnesota writer who is part Native American?

A: Louise Erdrich?

O: Yeah. Richard Ford.

A: What other books did you read as a kid?

O: A lot of sports books, or at least sports stories. I think there's an author called Matt Christopher. I also liked the S.E. Hinton books, like *The Outsiders* and *That Was Then, This is Now* and *Tex* and *Rumble Fish*. I really loved all of those. And then *A Separate Peace*. I remember, as an adult, grabbing that off the shelf and wondering if this holds up, and boy does it hold up.

A: What about in high school?

O: There were some books that were just *incredible* page-turners for me. *Lonesome Dove* I remember reading at military school, and turning out the lights to go to sleep and then just kind of sitting there and being like, 'No, I've got to keep going.' [laughs] And then reading it again. I think all this stuff you read as a kid really seeps into your consciousness: you know what a story is, or how you tell a story. And I really think that even though I never really studied acting or screenwriting, I think the foundation of reading so much as a kid... that maybe I entered into that Malcolm Gladwell 10,000-hour territory, where somehow I might have absorbed, as I said, a sense of story. And just developed an ear for language and dialogue that I really think helped me a lot with acting also, because I was lucky enough to work with directors who were very open to me, if I had an idea or a way of saying something.

A: You're kind of known for extemporaneity, for improvising.

O: They always say 'improvising' but it isn't 'improvising' in the sense of — it's not like, while we're talking I didn't plan on saying this, it just comes out... In my case it was more often the deal that I'd be studying the script and think of something. 'Oh, OK, maybe I'll try this,' then, you know, run it by the directors or the writers.

Wilson's bookshelves, while neat, don't adhere to any particular organisational scheme.

A: Can you give an example?

O: I just remember that line in *Wedding Crashers* where I say, 'You know how people say we only use ten per cent of our brains? I think we only use ten per cent of our hearts.' That's one of the things, the series of things, that we're saying to girls in that movie. But that line, I thought of it a month after we had filmed those scenes but when I told David [Dobkin], he was like, 'Yeah, that's pretty good. Let's go back and film it.' So we just added it in.

A: That is a good one.

O: There are some lines that will come up again and again and it'll be something that I would have gotten from my dad. I remember my dad describing this place in Dallas — this kind of run-down hamburger place he went to — as 'where dreams go to die'. That always stuck in my mind and I've used it a couple of times. And then I remember my dad saying to us, when he was frustrated with me and my two brothers, 'Never in my wildest dreams did I imagine that I would have children like this.' We gave it to Bill Murray in *Rushmore*.

A: Oh right, that's the greatest line.

O: In fact, the speech that Bill Murray delivers in *Rushmore* about rich kids — 'Take dead aim on the rich boys; get them in the crosshairs and bring them down' — was my dad. My dad would rail against inherited wealth. We went to a kind of, not fancy, but a private school in Dallas where a lot of the kids were well off, and that was one of my dad's big things. So when Wes and I were working on that and we needed to have Bill Murray deliver this speech there in assembly, we asked my dad. He wrote the whole speech.

A: So did you just say, like, 'Dad, what you would say about a bunch of rich kids?'

O: Yeah. 'Dad, there's this scene where we want Bill Murray to say something about rich kids, and, you know, our hero is not that, and we want him to kind of perk up as he's listening to this guy,' and that's what my dad said back to us.

A: I heard that you and Wes Anderson met at the University of Texas at Austin.

O: We took a playwriting class together.

A: So was he an English major too?

O: Wes was a philosophy major.

A: Did you guys talk about books?

5. BOTTLE ROCKET
—
The 1996 film about a trio of amateur criminals was the first movie collaboration between Wes Anderson and the Wilsons. 'The performers look like they're having a lot of fun,' said *The Hollywood Reporter* in a pretty good early description of Wilson's overall charm, 'but there is a great deal of skill on display.'

O: Yeah, certain books that we were both really into. One book that was a big thing to Wes and me, when we were in school, were those short stories Michael Chabon wrote that became his collection *A Model World*. There was one called 'Ocean Avenue' that we really liked. And we both would have been into Salinger.

A: When you and Wes then wrote together, would you say, 'Oh, read this,' or, 'Watch this...' Did you use a lot of references?

O: Yeah, that's what makes it so fun, writing with someone, or writing with Wes — a lot of our time was just spent sitting around and talking. And, you know, telling stories from stuff that happened, or something that we had observed, or read about, and seeing what could be used from that. Here's an example of something from *Bottle Rocket*. We were told we had to add a new scene because it tested so bad. So we added a scene of Luke leaving the insane asylum, and we've all done this escape — my character is freeing him — but his doctor comes to see him and he's like, 'But you could just leave.' He goes, 'I know, but he's figured out all this stuff.' That idea, I think, might have come from *Huckleberry Finn*, the part that people sort of dismiss when Tom Sawyer shows back up, and they're freeing Jim and doing all this stuff. Tom hasn't told Huck and Jim, who's already free, and that idea of doing stuff when you didn't need to do any of it — I'm sure that had its genesis in that *Huckleberry Finn* sequence.

A: Do you guys still write together?

O: No. We haven't written in forever. And the thing that I was just in France for, that Wes is doing now, I think he wrote that himself. I don't think he had a co-writer on that.

A: You're in a new movie of his?

O: Yeah, it's called *The French Dispatch*. I just have a small part, but that's the thing he has been working on. We're filming in Angoulême, which is near Bordeaux.

A: I read online, who knows if it's true or not, that *Huckleberry Finn* is your favourite book.

O: I think that would be. Or *The Great Gatsby*.

A: *Huckleberry Finn* is a good book to have as your favourite. They are both those sorts of books that are classics and it's like, 'Oh, *Gatsby*, we all read it in high school,' but you read *Gatsby* and it's perfect.

O: It really is. Sometimes I wonder how much I've really progressed or advanced from when I read those books, that those would still be my favourites. Certainly they're great books, but I think it might also be a reflection that I should be reading more literature instead of reading another World War II book. Antony Beevor on the fall of Stalingrad. Or something. But I just get into those books.

A: When do you read?

O: I read at night. I do like the feeling — and I'm probably becoming a bit like my dad — I like to have books stacked up around me. I like going back to Dallas. My mom is in the house that I grew up in and there's a guest house that wasn't there, but a lot of the books that are in there are stuff that was either on our shelves, or my dad's, or books of hers. So I just like going back. You know that feeling when you have a great book and you're out at dinner and you're thinking, 'Oh, it's going to be fun to get home and read'? I get that sometimes when I go home. Even though it's like, 'OK, now I'm going in to go to sleep,' I'll look at the shelf, and it's like, I'm going to take this, this and this [he motions like he is pulling books from a bookshelf] and I'm going to stack 'em up, and I'm going to read a little bit. And that's a bit how I tend to watch movies; I could voyage out and watch something new, where I don't *know* how it's going to be, or I could go watch, you know, this *Godfather* again, where I know I love it. I tend to do that, sometimes, with books: go back and get stuff that I've already read. I'll remember a passage that I want to try to find. Or sometimes just enough time has passed that, now, being fifty, it *is* kind of like a new book.

A: I don't remember a lot of stuff I read before twenty-five, honestly.

O: I went in yesterday to that other room, where my mother stays when she visits, and I brought a book in there and I was going to read, but then I saw this Lindbergh biography [*Lindbergh* by A. Scott Berg] that I had read *years* ago, and I was like, 'Oh, let me look at this'... and then that made the trip back into this room.

A: I see it, right there, on the nightstand.

O: Yeah. I hadn't read that book in so long. But I know he's buried in Maui, and I wanted to read, again, what he thought about Maui.

A: What's Maui like? I mean, I've been to Maui once, a few years ago, but what's your place there like? Do you go there to surf?

O: I do surf. I stand-up paddle-surf.

A: How much time do you spend there?

O: A few months a year. I live on the North Shore, in Paia. It's gotta be like the yoga capital of the world, a lot of holistic stuff, vegan food and acupuncture.

6. LINDBERGH
—
Charles Lindbergh, 1902–1974, was an American hero aviator, famous for his record-breaking solo flights, the media frenzy around the tragic kidnapping and murder of his infant son in 1932, and for his isolationist campaigning pre-WW2. Philip Roth, in his 2005 novel *The Plot Against America*, imagines Lindbergh as a historical proto-Trump figure who uses his celebrity to be elected President and negotiate a peaceful alliance with Nazi Germany.

7. EREWHON
—
Chain of exorbitantly ex-
pensive and outrageously
healthy grocery shops
sprawled throughout
the greater Los Angeles
area. Past patrons include
Sidney Poitier, Kim Kar-
dashian (as well as Kris,
Kourney, Kendall, Kylie
and Kanye), and Jessica
Biel. Their mysteriously
named 'Traveler Coffee'
is priced at a smidge
over $31.

A: Are you into hippy new age stuff or not so much? No judgement, because I am.

O: I don't totally get on board with the philosophy but I'm always interested in any sort of healthy eating. The grocery store in Paia, Mana, makes Whole Foods look like Kroger. Grocery stores are like bookstores for me. I can get excited about a good grocery store. Usually if you've spent twenty minutes in a conversation with me, it'll somehow turn toward Erewhon.

A: Have you read Joan Didion's writing about Hawaii, or W.S. Merwin's poetry?

O: I met Merwin, because my mom photographed him. We had lunch together, and then, this past summer, he was in the hospital and I went and visited him, and they said he'd like somebody to read to him. So I went, and he didn't want me to read to him. But I did just sit there, and we had a nice visit. He was sort of in and out. And I remember him kind of grabbing my hand, and he said, 'Oh, you're a good friend for coming by.' But he really didn't know who I was. He certainly didn't remember that we'd had lunch, but it was a touching thing. I visited him again at his house, when he got out of the hospital, and then he seemed irritated that I was there. In fact, he asked me why was I there. [laughs]

A: Was that in the last year, before he died?

O: That was this past summer and he was very sick and not very lucid. I've read a few of his poems. There's one I really like, '... I will try to wait for you on your side of things'. My mom showed me that.

A: When I was thinking about this interview, I remembered an essay by Nora Ephron in which she said that she can recall exactly where she was — what couch she was sitting on — when she read a particular book. Like: Doris Lessing on a corduroy couch; Mario Puzo on a purple slip-covered couch. Do you have that kind of memory?

O: I can do that sometimes with a movie, in the theatre, a little bit with a book. I definitely have a good memory for — but everyone must be like that? — something that really strikes you as good. I just like reading something over and over that I really like, and committing it to memory.

A: What's a book you've read like this?

O: I like the Frederick Exley book, *A Fan's Notes*. There are some great passages in there. I like the part where Mr Blue is telling him about working, selling aluminium siding. He has this guy working for him, a black guy, and he says something slightly racist or something,

Top left to bottom right: Pitt Rivers Museum, Bridgeman Images, WENN Rights Ltd/Alamy Stock Photo, Fox Searchlight/Kobal/Shutterstock, Pictorial Press Ltd/Alamy Stock Photo, Photo by Focus on Sport/Getty Images, The Print Collector/Print Collector/Getty Images, John van Hasselt-Corbis via Getty Images, Everett Collection Inc/Alamy Stock Photo, Found Image Holdings/Corbis via Getty Images, LMPC via Getty Images

ver for *A Moveable*
ast (p. 11)

Wilfred Thesiger's travelling party (p. 13)

Don and Betty Draper in *Mad Men* (p. 25)

rien Brody, Jason Schwartzman and Owen
ilson in *The Darjeeling Limited*

Elvis Presley in his bedroom (p. 11)

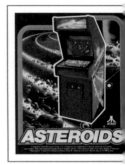

Asteroids poster (p. 14)

enny McLain of the
etroit Tigers (p. 30)

The island of Maui (p. 21)

Shakespeare and Company bookshop (p. 28)

ilson reads a self-help book (p. 24) in *The Haunting*

Typical Dallas postcard (p. 10)

Poster for *Shampoo*
(p. 24)

and then Mr Blue's not sure how what he said landed with Exley, so he covers his tracks and Exley says he gave his words 'the semi-humorous and cowardly twist men do when they're not sure they can enlist one on the side of their melancholy ignorance'.

A: What do you think is the underlying pleasure of rereading?

O: I think it's like a great story. When there's a great story that happens — I'm sure you have this, when something has happened with your friends — a story isn't good once. When you get together, a story is good over and over and over. A story that my brother and I might laugh at, something that my dad did — it's good once a year at least. Bring back that story and tell it.

A: And you do that with movies too?

O: Some. So, when you're flipping through, you'll see a movie and you'll stop and start watching it for a little bit... Do you have DirecTV? Five hundred channels. So you'll see a movie and you'll stop and start watching it for a little bit...

A: There are some movies that always seem to be playing.

O: There are some that *never* seem to play! And you're like, why isn't that ever on?

A: Where is *Rushmore*!?!

O: Yeah. Where's *Shampoo*! Why can't we ever see *Shampoo*!

A: Something I wanted to ask is whether you have any guilty reading pleasures: self-help, Tom Clancy, sci-fi, mysteries?

O: Self-help would be very guilty.

A: Well, biographies can be kind of like self-help.

O: Yeahhhh, but I'd be feeling much guiltier to have you come over and see, you know, *The Untethered Soul* by my bed. [laughs]

8. NO ONE HERE GETS OUT ALIVE

—

Famous biography of Jim Morrison. Apparently when asked in 1965 what his band would be called, the singer's answer was, 'The Doors. There's the known. And there's the unknown. And what separates the two is the door, and that's what I want to be. Ah wanna be th' dooooorrrrr.'

A: Do you have it? I have it. My stepmother gave it to me.

O: I don't know why I cringe a little bit with self-help in a way that I wouldn't with a biography — although I can get into reading, like, *No One Here Gets Out Alive*, or the Mötley Crüe Nikki Sixx book. Or one of the Guns N' Roses guys.

A: One of them wrote a book? I did not know that.

O: One of them did. Yeah, so I can get into those books. But it wouldn't be that you would want to lead with that, for one of those Proust Questionnaires: *What are you reading?* But I wouldn't feel guilty about any mysteries. You know, I got that John Le Carré book, *The Pigeon Tunnel*. It's his memoir and it's really great. And his father, Archie, was kind of a conman. I feel like there's a whole genre. Geoffrey Wolff wrote that book that I always love, *The Duke of Deception*, about *his* dad, who was kind of a complete conman. I have a soft spot for a great conman. I find that to be an interesting character.

A: It sure is.

O: I find them attractive in some ways. They say a really good conman is incredibly susceptible to other cons because they're dreamers, and to be really effective they've got to be able to sweep you up in their delusion or in their con — and to do that in a really convincing way they almost have to believe it themselves.

A: Do you ever feel like that, like all of us, you don't have enough time to read?

O: It's a little bit of a competition with TV, for me. I love watching TV, which I kind of blame on my parents because they got rid of our television for two years. It's like what Albert Brooks says in that movie, *Defending Your Life*: 'You *can't* take away TV — that's like taking heroin away from someone! You can't take TV away.'

A: All the young people I've known whose parents took away TV were just obsessed with it.

O: Well, I went through a long period of *never* watching TV — of course I watched too much sports — but that was before this Netflix/Apple TV thing happened. And *Mad Men* was the first that I was like, 'Hmmm, people are saying this is very good, OK, let's see.' I just ended sitting up even in that first episode, and being sort of surprised. Like, 'Gosh this is really good.'

A: I loved *Mad Men*.

O: I found that very literary.

A: It was like a novel. It really was. There were all these literary references in it too. Everything from *Gatsby* to Betty Friedan.

O: Jon Hamm I'd never seen before, so to me he was just Don Draper. I never had any problem where I go, 'Oh well, I've seen this actor in three other roles, and now he's playing this role.' It's like, 'Here's Don Draper, and this is a real person.' And then, you know, maybe my favourite character was Slattery.

A: I was going to guess Roger. I loved Betty, too. January Jones just wasn't playing the character to be liked at all.

Wilson is a member of the 'Frat Pack', a group of highly-bankable comedy actors that also includes Ben Stiller, Vince Vaughn and Owen's brother, Luke.

O: You know, when you got to Betty and the drinking and the being out in the suburbs, that felt like Cheever territory.

A: That was one of Matthew Weiner's influences — he said that in an interview in *The Paris Review*.

O: It had to be. Isn't there something they say happens to your brain, with reading, that they can tell with brain imaging, that doesn't happen with even something like watching *Mad Men*? Is that true?

A: Yeah, yeah. They've found it increases activity in parts of the brain related to language, whereas TV-watching lowers verbal ability, at least in kids. I always just feel less down when I read.

O: That's what I think. Sometimes, you know, you can feel isolated, and it's a good feeling to know that no matter how lonely you get you could always go read some of these great books. Ed Ruscha — do you like his work?

A: I do.

O: I got a book from him of *On the Road*. With photographs — it's in Malibu, I wish I could show it to you. But anyway, I think that's a little bit of him thinking about what's happening to books. The disappearance of books. That's an Ed Ruscha [he points to a long, horizontal blue painting on the back wall of his bedroom].

A: Oh, it is! That's beautiful. Do you collect a lot of art?

O: I do. I do. I really like Ed Ruscha. My mother photographed him. But I actually met him for the first time in Las Vegas, your stomping ground, at a Rolling Stones concert. He was there with Tony Shafrazi. I became friends with Tony Shafrazi and through Tony became friendly with Ed and then his wife, Danna. Ed's wife Danna would come over when Tony would visit me sometimes, in Malibu, and we would watch *Breaking Bad* or *Mad Men* together.

A: You've done a few movies that were based on books. *Wonder* was a book. *Permanent Midnight*. What else? *Breakfast of Champions*. When you prepare for movies like these, do you read the books?

O: I haven't. None of those! [laughs]

A: Do you ever read to prepare for a role? Or read other things adjacent to the role? Or is that not how one prepares for acting?

O: That might be how *one* prepares, but not this one. [laughs] But, you know, Ben [Stiller], when we're doing our press junket stuff, Ben will say, 'Owen likes to keep it fresh by *not* reading the script,' which isn't true. Ben [whispers] can be a little bit of a workaholic.

I more just kind of draw on reading the story, and, like I said, I might get an idea for, 'Oh, it might be good to try this.' Even working on *Midnight in Paris*, Woody Allen was not married to the script or getting every word perfect.

A: In that movie, your character was meeting up with these famous literary or historical figures: Hemingway, Fitzgerald, Zelda, Picasso, Gertrude Stein. Did you research them or read about them?

O: Yeah, there's something I say to Hemingway or Fitzgerald that I knew from reading about those guys. It's when I'm sitting with Hemingway, and I ask him to read my book, and he's going to give it to Gertrude Stein. He asks me if I like Mark Twain, and I say, 'I think you can make the case that all modern American literature comes from *Huckleberry Finn*.' Somehow, that's the reference that came to mind. It's true that that quote is a real Hemingway quote.

A: Paris, that's a good book city. Did you go to the bookstore Shakespeare and Company?

O: Of *course*, of course. And I know Sylvia, who took it over from her dad. What was her dad's name? George, who I met, sort of towards the end. I had known the store from Wes living in Paris and me going to Paris. I love going in, and I love how they let kids live there.

A: I know, right?

O: Isn't that great? They call them 'Tumbleweeds'. In exchange for the room, they'll work at the store. I'm always asking her, 'If you ever hear of an apartment, kind of right around there...' And so she is somewhat on the lookout for me. Then there's a bookstore, maybe within ten blocks of Shakespeare — I don't want to be disloyal but Shakespeare does such good business — called The Abbey. It's run by a Canadian guy. Very different, you can't even sit down, it's so crowded, just teeming with books. I told you that I got into *Arabian Sands*, and then I heard there was a biography on that guy, Wilfred Thesiger — and I can go there and ask the guy, and, sure enough, he's got it. So that's nice, when somebody can find everything and also seems really knowledgeable.

A: I love that.

O: And then there's a very good upscale bookstore on the Rue de Rivoli, next to the Hôtel Le Meurice. What's the name? Librairie Galignani. That's a *great* bookstore, where you *can* sit down.

A: What about bookstores in the US?

O: There's a bookstore here that I *love*, Angel City Books. It's

9. ANGEL CITY BOOKS
—
218 Pier Avenue
Santa Monica
CA 90405
Open from 11.30am to
6pm, seven days a week.

where I found *The Snow Leopard*. So many books that I have lying around here, I probably got from there.

A: Where is that?

O: That's right down on Main Street in Santa Monica. It's a second-hand store, and this guy, Rocco is his name, he's great. In fact, he gave me this picture right here. He made it for me.

A: 'Enjoy Every Sandwich.'

O: When he had some health problems, I said that to him — 'You've got to enjoy every sandwich' — which is from Warren Zevon. And he got a kick out of that and made this for me.

A: That's pretty good. I was wondering which artist made that.

O: I've talked to him a number of times, because I have such a good feeling at this store, about somehow having an office up there — there's a second storey — because I just like being around there. I always have a fantasy about having a bookstore, but I wouldn't want the pressure or any obligation or stress to sell or — you know, 'You gotta make this amount of money for rent.' I basically want that bookstore to always be there with that guy. That's what I want. And I'm desperate to keep that. Now bookstores are — sometimes they're just gone. You go, and they're gone.

A: It's so sad. What would your ideal bookstore be like?

O: You know that museum in Philadelphia where you have to make an appointment? The Barnes. Well, they changed it, but it used to be in his home and was displayed exactly according to his very eccentric specifications. That would be the model for my bookstore, and it would be appointment only.

A: I really love that you're looking to live near and above various bookstores. In Paris and this one.

O: I didn't even notice that until you pointed it out.

As the interview starts to wind down, he goes to his bookshelves and begins pointing out various books.

A: Is there any system?

O: No, they're just put in here. Talk about how a bad book can drag down a whole bookshelf.

A: Do you have some bad ones?

O: I think I do. Any book I get I'm not throwing out. I was really

10. THE BARNES
—
The Barnes Foundation museum is no longer appointment-only, but true to the wishes of its very particular founder, Albert C. Barnes, opens to the public only two days a week. Visitors can view the largest collection of Renoirs in the world, and 69 Cézannes - more than in all of France.

living in Malibu for ten years, so I wish we were doing this there — that's where most of my books are. And my dad gave me a lot of first editions, so I have some good ones. But most of them are packed away because of the fires.

A: Which are your favourites here?

O: Kingsley Amis — that makes me think of Martin Amis, and I love that collection of essays, *Visiting Mrs Nabokov*. He does one essay on darts, and talks about how darts is forever trying to escape the pub — its low origins — and become a little bit more refined. They go to the championships, which are in the Netherlands, and Martin Amis says that he is kind of comforted to see that 'the human butter mountain isn't a body type unique to England'. Isn't that good, 'the human butter mountain'?

A: That's funny.

O: *The Second Tree from the Corner* by E.B. White makes me think of my dad. He was a big E.B. White person, and his first cousin, Chip McGrath, was the fiction editor of *The New Yorker*. 'The Second Tree from the Corner' is one of my favourite short stories. I love that first line: 'Do you ever have any bizarre thoughts?' Here he's seeing the analyst, and he thinks, What thoughts *other* than bizarre thoughts has he had since the age of five? [laughs]

A: You have a great memory for quotes. And a lot of nice art books.

O: David McCullough — I was just in Panama, like I said, and he wrote a book about the Panama Canal, *The Path Between the Seas*. He was friendly with my parents and they had some book signings for him in Dallas. He wrote a book on the Brooklyn Bridge, and gave us a tour of it one time.

A: Oh, that's amazing.

O: And then I like this guy, speaking of conmen, Denny McLain. He was the last thirty-game winner in the major leagues, and then has kind of run afoul of the law since his big-league career. I was watching a documentary on him where someone — I don't know if it was his agent or a friend — said the thing with Denny is you could offer him two equal stacks of a million dollars: Stack A you can just take, Stack B you have to lie and cheat to get, and he'll pick Stack B.

A: [laughs] You do have a lot of biographies.

O: A lot of these I haven't read. There's a good Larry McMurtry memoir, *Walter Benjamin at the Dairy Queen*. It's one of those that have been lying around and I read it in the last year.

Image: Granger, NYC/TopFoto

A: And what's on your nightstand? I feel like I must look.

    O: Inside the Third Reich. Lindbergh.

A: *The Plague. Ed Ruscha's Los Angeles. The Spy Who Came in from the Cold.* That's a good stack there, and there are some really beautiful old covers.

    O: When I was just in Paris, a friend gave this, *Citizen Emperor* [Philip Dwyer] to me because I was like, 'I'd like to read a good Napoleon book.'

A: Oh, there's *The Collected Stories of Ernest Hemingway.* And *Gatsby*! *The Myth of Sisyphus.* [We both laugh.]

    O: I got that from Angel City Books.

A: I read somewhere that Ben Stiller said that you have 'a library in your mind'. Does he mean that you have a lot of literary references or cinematic references?

    O: He'll say that I have a really good memory for stuff that happened to us that he might have forgotten. Maybe that's what he's talking about. One time, when we were working together, I think on *Starsky & Hutch*, he started to feel like I was putting on airs by the books I was carrying around on the set. So then he started to carry around a book that was, like, almost an atlas-sized book.

A: That's so funny, to think of you guys playing those particular characters and doing that.

    O: I guess he thought I was being pretentious. [laughs]

AMANDA FORTINI is a writer who divides her time between Livingston, Montana, and Las Vegas, Nevada. She has written for *The New York Times*, T: The *New York Times Style Magazine, The New Yorker, California Sunday,* and *Vanity Fair,* among other publications. She thinks that *Rushmore* is as perfect a movie as *The Great Gatsby* is a book, and was happy to spend an afternoon talking about them both.

There's something
about the LA light.
Photographic assistance:
Tigran Tovmasyan.
Styling: Caroline
Newell. Grooming:
Karo Kangas.

RE-READING LIST

In a phone call after the interview, Wilson recommended eight books that offer nourishment no matter how many times they are devoured.

THE SECOND TREE FROM THE CORNER (1954)
E.B. White

Essays, poems and short stories by the prolific *New Yorker* contributor. Says Wilson: 'My dad was hopeful one of us would get into Dartmouth College, where E.B. White went, and when he found out my transcript was going to show that I was expelled from St. Mark's, we chose a quote from [White's novel] *Stuart Little*, "Live and learn." I think my aunt came up with this.'

THE GREAT GATSBY (1925)
F. Scott Fitzgerald

'The way Fitzgerald describes the smile of Gatsby is just great. When Max Perkins [Fitzgerald's editor] first read the initial draft, he wrote back and said, "You've described Tom Buchanan so well I could recognise him on the street, and would cross the street to avoid him. But I don't have such a clear image of Gatsby." I think that then compelled Fitzgerald to go back and do that description of Gatsby's smile as "one of those rare smiles that you come across maybe four or five times in your life," one that focuses on you "with an irresistible prejudice in your favour." When my grandmother, who I was very close to, passed, I quoted that, because I felt that she had an irresistible prejudice in my favour.'

SEYMOUR: AN INTRODUCTION (1963)
J.D. Salinger

'Of course, *The Catcher in the Rye* was huge for me as a kid, but that's almost like saying "Satisfaction" is your favourite song from The Rolling Stones. *Seymour: an Introduction* is more of a deep cut. I like that part where Seymour and his brother are in their apartment, and their father comes to visit. He's in a bad mood. He won't take off his overcoat and is glaring at things and all of a sudden gets up and goes to the mantlepiece and looks at a picture of their mom, his ex-wife, who I guess is gone, and turns and asks Seymour, "Do you ever remember riding on Joe Jackson's bicycle?" Joe Jackson was the trick rider in the circus, where his parents performed when they were young. And Salinger writes that Seymour answered him, "the way he answered all questions from their father, as if they were the questions he most wanted to be asked in his life." He replied: "I don't think I ever got off that bicycle." And then he says "aside from its enormous sentimental value to my father, this answer was true, true, true."'

THE SPORTSWRITER (1986)
Richard Ford

Third novel by the Pulitzer-winning author. 'I like the part where he runs into this guy, Walter Luckett, at a bar. He talks about the other times he's run into him. And he says, There's one time when he sat down, and after we exchanged a few things, it went into this horrible silence of us just *staring* at each other—it went on for five minutes or so until he got up and left without saying a word.'

ADVENTURES OF HUCKLEBERRY FINN (1885)
Mark Twain

'I love the part where Huck and Jim get separated on the raft. There's a storm and now the storm's kind of over, and it's still not quite dawn, and Huck gets back on the raft, and then decides that he's going to play a joke on Jim as it gets light. Jim's like, "My God, you're here, you're back!" And Huck's like, "What are you talking about?" And he's like, "We got separated," and Huck's like, "I've been here the whole night — you must have had a dream." And he's like, "How could I dream all of that?" And he's like, "Well you did because I've been here." And he's like, "That's the most powerful dream I've ever had, cause it was SO REAL!" And when he finds out Huck tricked him, he says that great thing to Huck that's just very powerful. He says, "I'm going to tell you what it means — it means this whole time when we were separated I was just so sad... and all you were thinking about was playing a trick on Jim."'

MIRACLE IN THE ANDES (2006)
Nando Parrado

True story about surviving a plane crash on a glacier. 'It's a first-person account by Nando Parrado, the guy who was responsible for getting them out. He lost his mom and his sister on the plane, and what kept him going was thinking about his father waiting, having lost his mother and his daughter. There's a spiritual element to the book that I appreciated. It's very moving.'

STALINGRAD (1998)
Antony Beevor

'Churchill has this quote about World War Two, that it was "won with American Money, Russian blood, and British courage." In *Stalingrad*, you see a lot of that Russian blood.'

THE SNOW LEOPARD (1978)
Peter Matthiessen

'There are books that I read in a day, which is just great—a page-turner—and then there are some that I enjoy so much I don't want them to end, and it seems like almost every page has something that's really meaningful on it, that I want to think about, to savour.'

THE STOIC
READER

Nature, exercise, philosophy, love: imperial life coach MARCUS AURELIUS and his secret diary that everyone's reading, the MEDITATIONS.

"Παρὰ τοῦ πάππου Οὐήρου,
τὸ καλόηθες καὶ ἀόργητον."

OPENING LINE

The *Meditations* were written in Koine Greek, which, along with Latin, was one of the official languages of the Roman Empire. The first line of Book 1 translates as: 'From my grandfather Verus: decency and a mild temper.' The author goes on to thank relatives, tutors and friends for traits including simplicity of living, moral freedom, and manliness.

Our Book of the Season for summer is an eternal best-seller, by a Roman emperor also known as the Philosopher. SEB EMINA traces how Marcus Aurelius's *Meditations* became the ancient world's most popular literary legacy.

SELF-HELP FOR ALL

Between the years 170 and 180 CE, Marcus Aurelius wrote a series of notes-to-self that would become known as the *Meditations*. They went on to be the most famous thing about him, which is astonishing when you consider that (a) they weren't intended for public consumption and (b) he was not only emperor of Rome but last of the so-called Five Good Emperors, meaning that the slow decline of the greatest empire on earth began, more or less, right after his death.

Eighteen hundred years have passed since Marcus Aurelius whiled away his reign fighting a series of far-flung frontier wars. More words are now published on an hourly basis than can be found in the entire surviving texts of antiquity. Many of these words are, like the *Meditations*, personal musings, moral judgements, motivational maxims, and so on. But Marcus's notes hold their own, showing as they do that even though everything has changed in most ways, nothing much has changed at all. As he himself fairly often puts it: 'all things have been the same kind from everlasting, coming round and round again' (2.14). Marcus's famous fans include J.K. Rowling, Arnold Schwarzenegger and Geri Halliwell. He is cited in rap lyrics and name-dropped in TED talks. There is a constant parade of activity dedicated to repackaging Stoicism, the ethical philosophy in which he partook, as the basis of a thriving modern self-help industry (so much for 2.16: 'the only lasting fame is oblivion').

The *Meditations* is a perennial bestseller, but not many people read it in the usual way. The twelve books into which it is divided consist of numbered entries, which don't invite the sustained completism of a novel or memoir. A common method is a kind of directed mindfulness: to open the book at random at the same time each day, often in the morning, and dwell on whichever insight is contained in a single entry. Is it a book at all, in the end, or just a particularly wise desk calendar? A Bible, without all the God stuff? Serious scholars will guide anyone truly interested in Stoicism to the work of Seneca and Epictetus, but Marcus Aurelius is more widely read, and perhaps that is to do with this bite-size format. Anyone can understand the *Meditations*. And despite the references to forgotten sports like quail fighting, the book has serious things to say about timeless subjects, especially that of identifying what a meaningful life might look like once you accept the inevitability of death. It makes you think, every time.

Marcus Aurelius wrote the *Meditations* in Koine Greek. Although they were in circulation during the centuries after his death, how exactly they survived is unknown. The first recorded mention occurs at the beginning of the tenth century. It is contained in a letter from the archbishop Arethas, who was influential in Constantinople, capital of what was left of the Roman Empire (and which we now call the Byzantine Empire). Writing to a friend, he says: 'I have had for a while now a copy of the Emperor Marcus's invaluable book. It was not only old but practically coming apart... I have had it copied and can now pass it on to posterity in better shape.' An unknown Byzantine poet wrote a composition entitled 'On the Book of Marcus' recommending that those who 'want to overcome sorrow' should read 'this blessed book' (recent Amazon reviews are similar).

The Turks conquered Constantinople

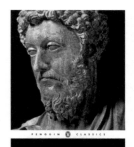

MARCUS AURELIUS
Meditations

in 1453 and Byzantine scholars fled to the West with chests and sacks of valued texts, the *Meditations* wedged somewhere among them. The Renaissance was triggered. The first printed version was published in 1559 and has been marketed under various titles ever since. In 1863, the English poet and critic Matthew Arnold described Marcus Aurelius as 'perhaps the most beautiful figure in history'. Why? Because he 'was the ruler of the grandest of empires; and he was one of the best of men'. Monarchs and presidents, quite keen to be beautiful figures in history, are fond of citing him, and it's comforting to think our leaders are aware that ethics and power aren't mutually exclusive, even if they don't always show it. Frederick the Great, who was king of Prussia, called Marcus Aurelius 'my exemplar and my hero'. During his presidential campaign, Bill Clinton named the *Meditations* when asked which book, aside from the Bible, had influenced him the most. The latter-day emperors who rule the world from Silicon Valley beanbags will often point to Stoicism as

a sort of secular faith. Marcus Aurelius is still affecting our world in ways we will never be fully able to trace.

The *Meditations* is a beautiful book, and a strange one. It fights its own frontier war: between philosophy and spirituality. It shows that philosophy isn't necessarily just word games and that spirituality needn't entail belief in supernatural beings. Despite being concerned with the fundamental questions of life and death, it's also very intimate. It's a private diary, after all. When Marcus refers to himself as 'you' he seems to be talking to himself, the whole of humanity and the individual reader, all at once. The atmosphere is a little like that of a horoscope. The ever-present 'you' invites the reader to ask, is this true of me? If so, how? If not, why not? Each time somebody opens the book and reads an entry, an entirely personal reaction is conjured up, such as those collected in the pages to come. So hurry up and read them. Book 4, entry 17: 'No, you do not have thousands of years to live. Urgency is on you.'

GYMNASIUM

It's good to have a sense of the meaning of life but what does that mean in practical terms? MASSIMO PIGLIUCCI shares three vital exercises for the everyday philosopher.

THE STOIC WORK-OUT

If you think of philosophy as just a modern academic discipline, populated by not particularly social PhD-holding characters who spend their lifetimes writing about the finer points of Kant's *Prolegonema to Any Future Metaphysics*, then the words 'practical philosophy' will sound rather oxymoronic to you. But this wasn't the case for most of the time, and in most places, in which philosophy has been pursued. The ancient Graeco-Romans actually *lived* their Epicureanism or Stoicism, just like the Chinese were doing with their Confucianism, or the Indians with their Buddhism.

1. WIFE
—
It's hard to know how much of the gossip about Marcus's wife, Faustina the Younger, was just political sniping. One persistent rumour was that Commodus, Marcus's son and successor, was the result of an extra-marital affair with a gladiator.

Marcus Aurelius, Stoic emperor, was one of the most practical philosophers the Western tradition has known. He presided over the Roman Empire for nineteen difficult years characterised by two frontier wars, an internal rebellion by one of his most trusted governors, a flood that inundated much of Rome, and a plague that killed close to five million people. Oh, and he had a notoriously philandering wife. If you think you are having a tough day, this may put things in perspective.

What helped him through these difficult times was his Stoic philosophy. Not because he managed to suppress his emotions and go through life with a stiff upper lip. If you think that's what a Stoic looks like, you are confusing the actual philosophy with one of those *Star Trek* episodes prominently featuring Mr Spock. Rather, Marcus put into practice a number of Stoic exercises, found in his famous book — known to us as *Meditations*, but which was actually his personal philosophical diary.

These and other philosophical exercises work according to a principle that has been confirmed and expanded by modern science. They represent a type of what is known today as cognitive behavioural therapy. The first step to tackle our problems, they assert, belongs to the realm of thought: we need to reflect on what is going on and, if necessary, acknowledge to ourselves that we should be pursuing a different course of action. Then comes behavioural modification: we have to nudge ourselves towards implementing a new behavioural pattern, no matter how odd or difficult it may initially feel. These two steps continuously reinforce each other, so that the new behaviour, constantly guided by cognitive analysis, eventually becomes second nature. Think of it as going to the gym: the first time you probably won't feel like doing it, everything will be awkward, and your muscles will be sore for days. But the more you repeat to yourself that this is good for you, and the more you do it, the more habitual it becomes, and your physical health benefits accordingly. The Stoic gym works in a similar way, only it is not your muscles but your mind and spirit that improve over time. It has worked for close to two and a half millennia, and it still works today.

Here are three of my favourite spiritual exercises from the *Meditations*. I find them particularly useful in alleviating the problems of twenty-first-century life. Which turn out to be not very different from the problems of second-century life, give or take a plague (for them) and the existence of social media (for us).

EXERCISE 1: TAKE ANOTHER'S PERSPECTIVE

7.26 When someone does you wrong, you should consider immediately what judgement of good or evil lead him to wrong you. When you see this, you will pity him, and not feel surprise or anger. You yourself either still share his view of good, or something like it, in which case you should understand and forgive: if, on the other hand, you no longer judge such things as either good or evil, it will be easier for you to be patient with the unsighted.

Imagine you have been waiting in line for quite a while at the bank. You finally make it to the counter, and the cashier informs you rather brusquely that the computers are down. You feel the outrage swelling inside you. How dare he treat you like that? After all the waiting you've done? You are the customer! Right, Marcus would say. But stop and think: have you never treated others brusquely because you were frustrated? After all, the cashier has been dealing with the situation for hours, taking the brunt of multiple customers' dissatisfaction.

When you find yourself in this sort of situation, first take a few deep breaths (from the diaphragm), so that you start to calm down and

THREE STOIC PRODUCTS (1)

can examine the situation more objectively. Then close your eyes and — as vividly as possible — imagine yourself in the cashier's situation. Finally, ask yourself if you wouldn't lose your patience a bit, just like he has done. Repeat to yourself (mentally if you are not alone; out loud if you are): 'He thinks he has a right to act that way. And you would too, if you were in his place. Bear, then, with patience. It will pass,' or a similar phrase of your own.

EXERCISE 2: PREMEDITATE ON ENCOUNTERING DIFFICULT PEOPLE

2.1 Say to yourself first thing in the morning: today I shall meet people who are meddling, ungrateful, aggressive, treacherous, malicious, unsocial. All this has afflicted them through their ignorance of true good and evil. But I have that the nature of good is what is right, and the nature of evil what is wrong; and I reflected that the nature of the offender himself is akin to my own — not a kinship of blood or seed, but a sharing in the same mind, the same fragment of divinity. Therefore I cannot be harmed by any of them, as none will infect me with their wrong. Nor can I be angry with my kinsman or hate him. We were born for cooperation, like feet, like hands, like eyelids, like the rows of upper and lower teeth. So to work in opposition to one another is against nature: and anger or rejection is opposition.

There is much wisdom packed into this quote. To begin with, it's a good thing to start your day, especially one you deem to be particularly difficult, by reminding yourself of the challenges ahead. This can be done by closing your eyes and taking a few minutes to visualise the likely scenario, or by writing out a description of the scenario in a few sentences. A prepared mind reacts better to new situations.

Notice also that Marcus is telling himself that, so to speak, we are all in the same boat, and that the best we can do is to work with each other, not to waste time and energy by indulging resentment towards others. To remind myself of this, I use a simple mantra: 'We are all members of the cosmopolis.' I repeat it several times, either to myself or out loud, whenever I encounter people who are difficult to deal with.

EXERCISE 3: DECOMPOSE YOUR DIFFICULTIES

8.36 Do not let the panorama of your life oppress you, do not dwell on all the various troubles which may have occurred in the past or may occur in the future. Just ask yourself in each instance of the present: 'What is there in this work which I cannot endure or support?' You will be ashamed to make any such confession. Then remind yourself that it is neither the future nor the past which weighs on you, but always the present; and the present burden reduces, if only you can

isolate it and accuse your mind of weakness if it cannot hold
against something thus stripped bare.

Ever felt overwhelmed by a multitude of current preoccupations and
tasks to be carried out, worries about the future, and regrets about the
past? You are in good company, of course. The Stoic position, however,
is that it is a waste of one's emotional energy to regret past events, since
they can no longer be changed. And that the best way to prepare for
the future is by paying attention to what we are doing here and now.

There are several techniques that come in useful in this respect, including one which I borrow from Buddhist meditation, only adapted to
the twenty-first century. During meditation it is common for random
thoughts to intrude into your mind. One way to deal with them is to
imagine that the thought is a leaf, visualise gently picking it up, putting
it on the surface of a stream and watching it drift away. My version
is to acknowledge the thought — say a feeling of regret for some past
action — and then gently 'swipe left' with my mind (or with my actual
hand, if I am alone). I then try to refocus my attention on whatever task
is at hand.

Another technique, this one to better deal with an ongoing, difficult task, is to ask myself (again, mentally or out loud): 'Do you think
nobody else in the world has ever had to deal with this? If they got
through it, why can't you?' Then I break the problem down into man-
ageable bits and start work on them, beginning with the items that are
more readily under my control, or where I think I can make the most
progress in the least time. This makes me feel better, reduces anxiety
and readies me for whichever steps I must then take.

MASSIMO PIGLIUCCI is K.D. Irani Professor of
Philosophy at the City College of New York. His books
include the newly-published *Live Like a Stoic*, as well as
Nonsense on Stilts: How to Tell Science from Bunk. He is
on the organising committee of the Stoicon conference,
which is in Athens this year on 5 October. He blogs at
patreon.com/FigsInWinter.

ROMA

Does a man's personal history have anything to do with
human history? Twenty-six years ago during a romantic break in Italy, GEOFF DYER encountered the
bronze Marcus Aurelius statue in Rome.

MEMORY IS A SOUVENIR

In late July 1993, I arranged to meet my on-off (more off than on)
Serbian girlfriend in Italy. I flew from London; Anja was coming from
Belgrade by train to Venice, where I promised to be waiting for her
at the station. This kind of arrangement was much more precarious
back then, with no mobile phones or internet, and I was conscious,
as I hurried into the station, that I was late. Fortunately her train had
been delayed so as she walked towards me along the platform, drinking
water from a bottle, I was able to watch her as though I had been waiting patiently for twenty minutes. She was almost my height, carrying

a large rucksack without being weighed down by it. Her black hair did not smell of train or travel. She'd never been to Venice before but, being Venice, it looked as it always had, as everyone has always expected it to look. We took a packed vaporetto across to Giudecca, where we had rented a room in a palazzo owned by an Englishman I'd been in touch with: an Airbnb-style arrangement before such a thing existed. The previous evening — for some reason I feel this is significant even if the nature of the significance is not clear — I had gone to see Nusrat Fateh Ali Khan at the Barbican Centre.

After three nights in Venice Anja and I went on to Siena and then to Montepulciano, where we had the most incredible luck. All the hotels were expensive, heavily booked and awful in that over-stuffed baroque style. We were then shown to a simple and cheap room with a white bed and an old terrace — formerly some kind of little bridge linking two buildings — overlooking the sizzle and stillness of Tuscan fields: a huge view that felt like a private view; four nights like a glimpse of for ever.

From Montepulciano we took a bus to Chiusi and then a train to Rome. Neither of us had been to Rome before. We walked from Termini to the apartment of my friend Michele Avantario, at <u>18 Via Venezia</u>, nervous about getting pickpocketed, sweating under our rucksacks in the scalding heat. Michele then drove us to the apartment owned by his girlfriend's mother where we would be staying. She was in France so we would have the place to ourselves, just off Campo De' Fiori. Our Roman holiday could not have been more Roman and it was hard to believe that Rome had ever been hotter. That night we went with a group of Michele's friends to eat pizza in Trastevere: a vast eatery with cool marble tables and fluorescent strip lights. It was devoid of atmosphere in any decorative sense but the atmosphere was still wonderful because it was jam-packed with people and laughter, talking and chewing. Later I learned that this famous pizza place was known as L'Obitorio: the morgue.

The morning after our evening at the morgue Anja and I walked to Campidoglio, climbing the steps towards the statue of Marcus Aurelius astride his horse, the statue which was the first thing that Joseph Brodsky noticed — from a taxi — on his first trip to Rome, as recorded in the essay 'Homage to Marcus Aurelius'. Anja, who had studied architecture in Belgrade, told me about Campidoglio, how it only looked like a perfect square because it wasn't. Michelangelo, she said, had designed it in such a way as to compensate for the foreshortening of perspective.

That was her contribution. Mine was to use this observation in a story several years later. More immediately, as we sat in a shrinking sliver of equine shadow, sheltering from the blazing sun, it was to take out my black-spined Penguin Classics copy of Marcus Aurelius's *Meditations*. As a narrative gesture that works conveniently enough but the truth is that we didn't think much of the book. I'm not being entirely serious when I say it's the worst kind of serious writing, but back then I wasn't in the mood for wisdom and am probably even less in need of it now, especially wisdom in *Do-this-don't-do-that-don't-do-this-do-that* form. Parts of it are like the philosophical thoughts recorded by Martin Sheen (Kit) midway through his killing spree with Sissy Spacek (Holly) in *Badlands*: 'Listen to your parents and teachers... Try to keep an open mind. Try to understand the viewpoints of others. Consider

2. 18 VIA VENEZIA
—
The building has since become home to a two-star hotel, the Hotel Italia, which has a TripAdvisor rating of 4.1 out of 5.

TOURISMS

All empires end up as holiday destinations. Four photographs by MARTIN PARR document the riveting theme park we know as Rome.

the minority opinion but try to get along with the majority opinion once it's been accepted.' When Marcus tells us to 'be like the headland against which the waves break and break: it stands firm, until presently the watery tumult around it subsides once more to rest,' I feel like Grasshopper listening to blind Master Po in an ancient episode of *Kung Fu*. (On this particular point, master, it's not such sound advice anyway since if one takes the long view — which is what philosophers have been doing for the longest time — the house perched on the coast with a panoramic sea-view window will eventually crumble into the tumult which had only subsided in the interests of securing long-term victory.) There's also a lot of *Desiderata*-type stuff — 'Go placidly amid the noise and the haste...' — that irks even if it's less irksome than when he's in signs-at-the swimming-pool mode: *No diving. No denim cut-offs. No bombing. No canoodling.* I don't like being bossed around and given instructions unless they're very clear and unambiguous instructions on how to use a kitchen appliance or how to work the TV in a hotel room (where, needless to say, such much-needed instructions are in short supply). When it comes to lessons in conduct *Middlemarch* is more my cup of tea than *Meditations* — though *Pronouncements* might be a better name for a book even Brodsky concedes is 'melancholy and repetitive'.

In turn I concede that there were some bits I enjoyed reading aloud to Anja. 'Do unsavoury armpits and bad breath make you angry?' We liked this because it sounded like a line from a classical advertisement, either for deodorant and mouthwash or for a course in anger-management — or Christianity as it was known back then. And he's sort of right — this is me now, rereading the book, aged sixty, in 2019, in Los Angeles — when he asks us to remember 'that man lives only in the present, in this fleeting instant: all the rest of his life is either past and gone, or not yet revealed'. I say 'sort of' because I still have a photograph of Anja lying naked on our terrace in Montepulciano and while it's true that I can't go back in time to the moment I took the picture — if I could I'd have asked her to open her legs more — part of who I have become (which may or may not be the same as who I have always been) is still defined by it, by having been there then, before leaving Montepulciano and going on to Rome and seeing the statue of Marcus and his horse where the light, the thing that anchored us in the moment, was absolutely unchanged since the Emperor himself was there in the flesh, back in AD whatever-it-was.

Later that afternoon I went with Michele when he had to drive to EUR to pick up a coffee table that he wanted me to take back to London for the friend who had first introduced us. En route we stopped at a café where he said to me, 'You 'ave to 'ave a girlfriend in every town, man,' and although this might not seem as wise as something Marcus Aurelius might have said I took it to heart because Michele Avantario's heavy Italian accent made it sound less like the coarse creed of a sailor than an expression of the immense romantic — *Roman*tic — promise of a world flooded, as this corner of it was, with light and heat. And jeez, was it ever hot. Stalled in traffic, the car's A/C struggling to cope, Michele said, 'Is 'ot, man!' as though it were atrociously hot even by the scorched-earth standards of Roman history. In the early evening he dropped me off near Campo de' Fiori where I saw Anja perched on the edge of a fountain, weighed down by the melancholy that you often notice in people when they are unobserved,

3. MELANCHOLY

—

Adds the author: 'The narrator of Nicholson Baker's footnote-crowded novel *The Mezzanine* has been carrying around the very same Penguin Classics edition "for two weeks of lunch hours"; "tired of Aurelius's unrelenting and morbid self-denial," he gives up on it entirely after a passage "about mortal life's being no more than sperm and ash."'

especially if they are waiting. With that in mind it occurs to me that waiting is not always future-orientated (waiting for something to happen or someone to arrive); you can also find yourself waiting *after* it has happened or they have gone. Melancholy, to reverse the same logic, can be in anticipation rather than in response.

After all is said and done Marcus Aurelius is right: you can only live in the present, but that only intensifies the desire to relive the past, especially days like those three in Rome, because back then, even though I lived them, I couldn't fully appreciate them as I can now when I can't even remember them properly. I didn't know then, for example, that L'Obitorio would set a standard for pizza by which every subsequent pizza experience would be judged for the rest of my life, though I would never have attained that knowledge had I not gone to L'Obitorio in the first place. If I *could* live those three days again, not a single moment would be wasted, because what does it matter, in the long run, if the fresh orange juice was outrageously expensive at the café in Campo de' Fiori where we had breakfast, the morning after pizza at L'Obitorio? All that matters is that I was in a foul mood as a result, because I was always paying for everything, before we set off for Campidoglio. Either way, the facts of the past remain unchanged. On 4 August I saw Anja off at Termini and then, the next day, I flew back to London with the irritating coffee table.

Later I lived in Rome with another girlfriend, in her apartment on Via del Moro in Trastevere. We must have eaten at L'Obitorio hundreds of times, occasionally twice in the same night, and we spent many evenings hanging out with Michele and other friends at the nearby Bar San Calisto. I've been back to Rome a couple of times with my wife, but the first time it poured with rain and the second time it was the middle of August, so L'Obitorio and the San Calisto were closed for the holidays, and Trastevere was overrun with tourists like us. The message from the gods was clear, even if there are no gods and the only messages are in the form of graffiti: you have had your time here and there is no point trying to repeat it.

Brodsky died in 1996, Nusrat in 1997; Michele died in 2003, and I have no idea what became of Anja. Unusually, I can find no trace of her on the internet, but if she is alive I know that, from time to time, she will think about those days and nights in Italy, and statistically it's highly likely that there are moments when we both think of them in the same way and — as happened when we met at the station in Venice — at exactly the same time.

GEOFF DYER is normally out of bed by 7.30am. His latest books are *The Street Philosophy of Garry Winogrand* and '*Broadsword Calling Danny Boy*' (on the film *Where Eagles Dare*). He is also the editor of a new selection of essays by D.H. Lawrence, *Life with a Capital L*.

ADDENDUM

'Don't just say you have read books. Show that through them you have learned to think better, to be a more discriminating and reflective person. Books are the training weights of the mind. They are very helpful, but it would be a bad mistake to suppose that one has made progress simply by having internalized their contents.' — Advice on reading by the Stoic philosopher Epictetus. The former slave was a significant influence on Marcus Aurelius, who became emperor shortly after his death.

INSECTUM

Marcus Aurelius was very fond of bee analogies: see 5.1 (ideal agents of nature), 5.6 (unselfconscious humility), 6.54 (public-spirited socialism) and 11.18 (gregarious goodness). Curious to test these notions in the arena of hard fact, HARRIET ALIDA LYE quizzes bee scientist Gro Amdam.

THE TRUTH ABOUT BEES

'What does not benefit the hive does not benefit the bee either' (6.54). Can the world of honeybees teach us how to be selfless? In the complex society of the hive, all citizens play a part to serve a common goal. Bees have been working their alchemy to turn nectar into gold for millions of years, and as their colonies have developed, so too have their democracies. As it turns out, bees aren't all subordinates in service of a dictator queen.

Gro Amdam is a Norwegian biologist working in Arizona who studies the origins of social behaviour in honeybees. She explains that worker bees are by definition altruistic: by living in the hive, they have given up the opportunity to raise their own babies in order to raise the queen's. But this does not mean that worker bees are powerless. I spoke with Gro over Skype to discuss feminist, worker-led bee democracies, hive dance floors, and what humans might learn from bees in order to operate better systems of power.

HARRIET: Can you tell me about the evolution of social behaviour in bees, and what it means to be social?

GRO: In all bee species it's the females that make up the social structure, whereas the males, which we call drones, don't work. They don't raise broods, they don't forage, they don't defend the hive. So when we talk about social behaviour in bees, we are really asking how females are social. When I started researching that question back in around 2000, there was this promise, or hope, that by sequencing the genome of honeybees we would learn a lot about what it means to be social. But I had some questions as to whether we could really have this expectation — if the genome would include exclusive genes devoted to being social — because the behaviours that

worker bees display in their division of labour are basically ordinary female behaviours that are usually expressed in any solitary-living female bee. You eat food, build a nest, forage specifically to provision the nest and care for your brood, and maybe repeat this if you could live long enough, and then at some point you die. So what the worker bees were really doing was taking these behaviours and dividing them up among a collective.

H: Are the workers and drones all equal beneath the queen, or is there a further and more complex hierarchy within the society of a hive?

G: We think of hierarchies as a decision-making pyramid, with an individual on top making decisions. The queen, certainly, with her pheromones and her behaviour, is the key to many decisions made within the hive. If the queen is healthy, that is certainly how it plays out most of the time. But in fact workers can make decisions that override the queen, and the worker democracy is more important than the queen and what she might be signalling. The queen is just going about laying eggs, and her pheromones are very important for the social cohesiveness of the colony, but queens can lose quality: the queen ages or there's

QUEEN

something else that happens to her so that her pheromones are perceived as less good by the workers, and that's when they might make a democratic decision to try to replace her. When the workers perceive this, some of them might start creating 'queen cups', where an egg can be reared into a queen larvae. However, some workers will disagree with that decision and they will try to tear these cups down. So you have some workers building queen cups, and others tearing them down. If there are more building — in other words if there's a majority opinion that there needs to be a new queen — then ultimately there will be a new queen. Worker bees also decide democratically where the colony should live, which is a very important decision. Whether to have drones in the colony or whether to kick them out, those are also worker decisions. Drones do not make any decisions — decisions are being made for them over their heads. Only females make decisions in the bee democracy.

H: How did the evolution of this democracy happen? Did bee democracy emerge with the development of the social structure?

G: Workers act based on local information — based on what they know from their immediate environment. No bee knows everything. Insects work based on what they can sense right there and then. That implies that to get a democracy, and make decisions together that we as humans perceive as 'intelligent', knowledge needs to be dispersed among individuals. Interestingly, social insects very often make the 'right' decision, so to speak — if humans know what the right answer would be, for example what the best place to live would be, the bees almost always figure it out based on very limited information. They have 98% accuracy. To disseminate the knowledge you need to somehow get this information to an arena, such that each individual piece of information that is local can become global. For example, when a colony is deciding on where to live and is in a state of wanting to swarm — they know this because of pheromones, so the entire colony knows that it is time — each different location is found by one worker. In order to communicate the location, she dances a dance — you know that they can dance for the locations of flowers, but they can dance for nests too. This is a dance of her local information,

WORKER

occurring on the 'dance floor' of the colony. The other bees can then fly out and check out that location, and if they like the nest site, they will dance too. Here's how the democracy works: the better the nest is, the bees that come back from that location will dance with great enthusiasm, whereas other nest sites explored by other workers will not get as much excitement, so there will be fewer dances. The colony is going to hold back on swarming until all the dances are for one particular place, meaning that there's consensus.

H: Do bees have personalities or individual characteristics of their own, or are they defined as a collective?

G: This is a very interesting question: the question is what is personality, do animals have personalities? If yes, what kinds of animals have personalities? What we can say for worker bees is that based on their prior experiences, or their environments, and their talents, which have a specific genetic component, you get a unique timeline of events and perceptions for individuals. I would say that as all workers have a unique experience as they go through life, so they have a unique substrate to develop a personality from. We can observe workers and start to understand that their behaviours are based on their experience, and that that's a form of personality. It's an individual propensity to act in a certain way that's informed by previous experiences and, to some extent, genetics.

H: What does humanity have to learn from the bees?

G: A lot of people are discussing now how there's a lot to learn from this bee democracy that I talked about. Decision-making

UNIVERSAL NATURE

'All that happens is as habitual as roses in spring and fruit in the summer. True too of disease, death, defamation, and conspiracy — and all that delights or gives pain to fools.' (4.44) Watery decay tinged with a sense of hope, frozen in a study by artist JOCELYN LEE.

DRONE

Previous page: *Dark Matter #6 (Sunflower and Sky)* , 2016 © Jocelyn Lee, Courtesy Pace MacGill Gallery

— but bees are able to take that process to the next level and make a collective decision, whereas we, at that point, think we need leadership to decide.

H: What do you think bees think about in their day-to-day lives?

G: As you know, there's a discussion around consciousness, and what we define as thought, and some would say that in order to say that an animal has thought they need to see some evidence of planning. In the examples I mentioned of honeybees and the decisions they make, it's not a 'plan', it's many hundred individuals that each do what they feel like in any moment, but because there are thousands of them, it seems like a plan that has a lot of thought and detail. We can ask bees what they feel like in a moment, and observe how they respond, but that's a very simple measurement of what they might be thinking. We are not pretending to know what they are thinking, but we can know what they are sensing, and what sort of biases they might have. I'm sure that we can learn about how they put things together, and what we could call their thought process; and to get to the bottom of that we need to learn what individuals have experienced so that we can understand where they're coming from when an opportunity is presented to them.

H: There's a lot of concern in the media about the decline of bees and their well-being in the current climate. Can you talk about that?

G: Bees can be wiped out by epidemics of diseases, which can be local to certain regions or more widespread. We have researched the potential to vaccinate queen bees so that they can vaccinate their larvae against very common and dangerous pathogens, and it would work in a similar way to how pregnant women can transfer immunity to their fetuses prior to the birth of the baby, through the blood barrier. If we vaccinate the beehives to keep pathogen levels lower, this is also going to help the wild bees because of the way germs are shared on flowers.

processes that are dependent on a strong leader — for example, military, corporate — are very sensitive, or you could call them lacking robustness, because they're dependent on a single person, and what that person is deciding or not. Sometimes that works out great, but other times it does not go so well. So in times of conflict, it's a very common strategy to go for the leaders: in knocking out the leadership group, everything else falls apart. But if you have a process where decision-making is distributed, and local decision-making leads to the correct answer and is robust, that's a kind of 'invention' in bee societies that is being given a lot of attention and is quite intriguing. The possibility of creating robust decision-making processes that are not based on a central decision-maker. Some processes in social media are examples of this, where lots of little entities can create events, so it's a distributed process that comes to fruition through the contributions of many.

H: In what way does social media create this distributed decision-making process?

G: Here is an example of this, but it also shows that we are not really there yet: the March for Science happened a while ago when people everywhere started to respond to a problem, and they wanted to say something, to express their concerns, they wanted action. Discussions were happening among groups, but at some point there was a call for leadership to step up and organise a certain day, and there was the formation of a core group of people who were making these decisions. That's when the process of decision-making becomes the centralised process we are used to. Social media is an opportunity to create a shared interface for having an experience, just like the dance floor of the bee colony

HARRIET ALIDA LYE is a writer living in Toronto. When she was researching bee life for her novel, *The Honey Farm*, she learned that in parts of China, where there aren't enough bees to pollinate crops, workers are hired to dust the flowers with chicken feathers.

A meditation completely remeditated, by novelist and playwright DEBORAH LEVY.

HELTER-SKELTER

6.13

How good it is when you have roast meat or suchlike foods before you, to impress on your mind that this is the dead body of a fish, this is the dead body of a bird or pig; and again, that the Falernian wine is the mere juice of grapes, and your purple edged robe simply the hair of a sheep soaked in shell-fish blood! And in sexual intercourse that it is no more than the friction of a membrane and a spurt of mucus ejected. How good these perceptions are at getting to the heart of the real thing and penetrating through it, so you can see it for what it is! This should be your practice throughout all your life: when things have such a plausible appearance, show them naked, see their shoddiness, strip away their own boastful account of themselves. Vanity is the greatest seducer of reason: when you are most convinced that your work is important, that is when you are most under its spell.

'All the same,' I said to Marcus, 'I need less common sense and clear-mindedness from you. Frankly you often come across as hostile. Not so much to me, though there is that, no, hostile to yourself.'

'I am clear-minded, it is true.' He smiled a hard, sad smile, and set about scoring the skin of two fleshy black bream with his penknife. He tossed the fish on the fire and then leaned back against the narrow trunk of the pine tree. 'You are my dreamer,' he said, 'you add colour to my existence. When I am with you on a Sunday, I am happy.'

'No, Marcus.' I spiked a stick through the bream to keep them from falling apart in the fire. 'You are your own dreamer, no one can dream for you.' We both watched a bird land and settle on a stone wall that could be described as a ruin.

'Give me an example of this hostility.' Marcus squeezed the tip of his elbow as if he were in pain. It was very erotic, the way he squeezed his elbow.

We had made the fire from kindling that had washed up on the shore. Marcus had insisted we carry it for three miles to the forest in which we eventually made love. There was plenty of kindling in the forest, but Marcus pretended not to notice.

'To get to the heart of the manner,' I smiled uneasily at my lover, 'I believe you suffer from a vague disabling despair disguised as strength.'

'Look,' he said, 'I promise I will never burden you with my anxieties, I will never share an abundance of feeling, or claim to be God, or discuss my allergies in your presence, or see monsters in the shape of the clouds, or be over-impressed with your cashmere coat, which, after all, is made from hair that once belonged to the underbelly of goats.'

'You are so rational you are slightly insane.' I kissed his tormented elbows and he in turn kissed my hand, which was still bloody from gutting the fish.

Earlier that afternoon, we'd had our palms read by a palmistry expert, Madame R, on the pier. While the waves crashed around the helter-skelter next to Madame R's palmistry booth, she explained how the hands drawn on the walls of prehistoric caves in Spain and France were rendered with all the major lines shown in meticulous detail. 'Humans have studied the lines on their hands since the Stone Age,' she said to Marcus, who wasn't listening. She located the lines of life on our up-turned palms, also the lines of the head, the lines of the heart and the lines of health. After a while, she told Marcus that it was likely, from gazing at the cartography of his hand, that his shoes were always lined up neatly under the stairs and that he knew his next three appointments without having to consult his diary.

'The hand,' Marcus replied testily, 'has twenty-seven bones, made up of fourteen phalanges on the fingers and thumb, five metacarpals connecting the fingers to the wrist, and I'm not certain, but it's likely that eight carpal bones make up the base.'

As Madame R prodded the parts of his thumb that she insisted were related to thought and will, we watched an adult man climb into a hessian sack to prepare for his journey down the spiral slide of the helter-skelter. Madame R charged us thirty British pounds for her palmistry services and told us we would live a long life.

Marcus was in a furious mood. 'If you were a cardiologist, Madame R, I would consider your fee a bargain.'

The sun was setting as I made a slash down each side of the fish, about one centimetre deep. Marcus was still in a rage with the palmistry guide.

He reached out and pressed my bicep. 'Please', he cried out to me as the pine trees turned orange and small animals frolicked in the foliage, 'I am ravenous. Let us eat these fat bream and drink our local wine.'

The succulent flesh fell away from the silver skin as we tore at the fish with our fingers. After a frenzy of devouring, Marcus popped the cork from the bottle of wine and drank heartily, before handing it to me. The wine was cool and aromatic. The fish was tender and salty. Birds were singing everywhere. The embers of the fire kept us warm as night drew in. Marcus held the white spine of the once fat bream in his right hand and gazed at it drunkenly.

'It's just a dead fish and you are mortal too,' he said.

'Yes, yes,' I agreed, moving closer to his lips as I tore off his shirt and pushed him down on to the soft, moist moss. In our sex play we stripped away the boastful selves we presented to the world and became something other. Marcus said, 'Tell me who I am and I will be him,' and I did tell him and we enjoyed his new self.

I was pleased, however, that he knew where he had put the car keys and that the tank was full of petrol. We drove through the small hours into Monday. I was also relieved that Marcus was a man who did not wish to be an eternal youth in a hessian sack sliding down a helter-skelter. We returned home speedily because he knew his south from his north.

DEBORAH LEVY's new novel, *The Man Who Saw Everything*, is published in August 2019. 'I received my copy of *Meditations*,' she says, 'while I was busy gutting two fleshy sea bream in my kitchen and listening to Laura Marling's gorgeous, uncanny song, 'Soothing'. Aurelius is not particularly soothing and neither is Marling.'

Image: Gianni Giansanti/Gamma-Rapho via Getty Images

Many of Rome's old imperial statues were melted down after the rise of Christianity. The statue in the Piazza del Campidoglio survived only thanks to Marcus being mistaken for the Christian emperor Constantine the Great.

THREE STOIC PRODUCTS (2)

It happens every day, so shouldn't we talk about it more? SADIE STEIN on why getting out of bed is such an impressive thing to do.

LEAVE ME ALONE

5.1

At break of day, when you are reluctant to get up, have this thought ready to mind: 'I am getting up for a man's work. Do I still then resent it, if I am going out to do what I was born for, the purpose for which I was brought into the world? Or was I created to wrap myself in blankets and keep warm?'

I didn't encounter the Stoics until I was sixteen, but a key pillar of their priorities was ingrained in me from a young age: that one should seize the opportunity to get out of bed in the morning with a zeal that borders on masochism. In my mother's family, getting up early was a competitive sport. When we spent summers with my maternal grandparents in Northern California, the day began at five. And since the earliest risers were given to shouting between rooms of their ranch house, this meant everyone's day started at five, whether we wanted it to or not. *Why* was never explained. It's not as if we were getting up to milk cows or feed chickens; no, everyone was just getting up to do nothing for the next sixteen hours. 'I was actually up at three,' my grandmother might say smugly as she mixed pancake batter. 'Really?' her son would ask. 'I didn't sleep at all.' Only my grandfather — whose room was set back from the others — refused to take part: he'd lie in until ten, at which time, one of us would bring him breakfast in bed. (But then, he was considered lazy and eccentric, and was obsessed with a vague, apocalyptic future happening known as the 'Bad Times'.)

The lasting appeal of Marcus Aurelius's writings can be partly explained by the fact that he bestows heroic meaning on quotidian things like getting out of bed: activities that we all do and that we have always done. In the case of emerging from sleep, clearly he understands that it is not merely a question of standing up and getting dressed but an essential struggle: between sloth and work; comfort and industry; avoidance and engagement; sin and virtue. It's the one bit of philosophising

every human being must do each day. Do we want to 'wake up' — live, if you like, in the most literal and basic sense — or disengage? 'Getting out of bed' is a phrase so redolent of depression that 'not getting out of bed' is a tick box on the diagnostic form. To get up early is — as we learn in America from a young age — to be healthy, wealthy and wise. And like so many bromides, we take it for granted and punish ourselves — and each other — when we fall short.

Those who wish to be propelled into the day without the indignity of reluctance may turn to an entire industry of tricks, varying from the gentle (lamps that lighten gradually so as to stimulate the body's circadian rhythm) to the punitive (immediately having a cold shower so as to head off any lingering ambiguity). My preferred method involves an alarm clock hidden across the room in my bathrobe's pocket. It's about the waking self of the night before successfully tricking the sleepy (and, implicitly, worse) version of the morning after. A friend of a friend, so I'm told, once went through a phase in which he would record himself delivering a speech each night and then set it to switch on the following morning: 'Hello. You think you don't want to get up, but I know best. I'm you.'

Marcus Aurelius's notes, from him to him, were essentially this method's pre-technology equivalent. 'When you are reluctant to get up from your sleep, remind yourself that it is your constitution and man's nature to perform social acts, whereas sleep is something you share with dumb animals. Now what across with the nature of each being is thereby the more closely related to it, the more in its essence, and indeed the more to its liking' (8.12). The trouble is, in 2019, the in-bed self can convincingly reply: what does it even mean to 'work with others' any more? Is staying in bed really so bad? It's certainly no great hindrance to productivity.

You can order yourself breakfast, keep in close touch with all your friends and family, and maybe pick up some new loungewear and bedding while you're at it. Want a housekeeper to wash all that? No need to move a muscle; there are, as the ads say, thousands at your fingertips. If you're bored, download the latest Tana French or binge on some cosy Netflix content — or maybe find someone to sleep with you or marry you, and some health insurance into the bargain. (You can also do a rigorous session of Pilates with a remote trainer.) Feel like hacking an election, or maybe stealing an identity? You're right where you need to be! Obviously you can work remotely; I'm writing this from the comfort of my bed right now.

Getting up is, in a literal sense, obsolete. Are we the poorer for it? A thousand years of wisdom would say yes. When the entire world arrives in your bed, are you free to stay there or are you, on some level, stuck in it, now that the old, great distinction between 'not up yet' and 'up now' is gone? Even as Silicon Valley titans boast of running their empires on two hours' sleep, they ensure that the rest of us can keep to our beds like the grandparents in Roald Dahl's *Charlie and the Chocolate Factory*.

I can't help thinking of my grandfather, the only one in the family who refused to bow to peer pressure, and was rewarded with daily breakfast in bed. Maybe he had it figured out all along. Or maybe the 'Bad Times' really were closer than we knew, and there just wasn't any real point.

SADIE STEIN is from New York, where she writes, lives, and cooks. While she's never embraced stoicism with her teenage fervour, she continues to regularly debate the moral imperative of arising from bed in a timely manner.

The *Meditations* is one of the oldest books fileable under 'self-improvement'. With the genre experiencing rocketing sales, its leading authors are asked a single question — about the qualities they have that are in fact immune to transformation.

TWELVE SELF-HELP GURUS IN NEED OF HELP

'Change: nothing inherently bad in the process, nothing inherently good in the result' (4.42). A consortium of leading self-help authors are asked: 'What is one thing about yourself — as in you, personally — that you can never change?' Their answers differ tremendously, embracing the personal and the universal, the pragmatic and the mystical, the limiting and the liberating.

ROSEMARY DAVIDSON
Author of *Craftfulness: Mend Yourself by Making Things*

'I'd like to become a 'morning person'. I have never been able to get up or go to sleep at what most people consider normal or sociable hours. I have become almost entirely nocturnal, falling asleep to the sound of the dawn chorus, which would be fine if I worked a night shift. I don't.'

————

GRAHAM ALLCOTT
Author of *How to Be a Productivity Ninja: Worry Less, Achieve More and Love What You Do*

'I believe I could change most things about myself — from my weird biases (with enough therapy or challenge), to my baldness (if I cared enough to have surgery). There's certainly lots that I'm working on, but I guess I'd have to say the obvious answer is my death. None of us can change that, but it's a good reminder that we're not here very long, nothing is permanent and every moment and experience should be savoured.'

_____

STÉPHANE GARNIER
Author of *How to Live Like Your Cat*

'My attachment to freedom, in all its forms. Like a cat! As it says on my tattoo: "For in truth, nothing has changed and everything has changed. Forever, I'm out of here. Forever, I'm a liberty-junky."'

_____

ROBERT POYNTON
Author of *Do Pause: You are Not a To Do List*

'I cannot change the way I make significant decisions. All the big decisions in my life have been instinctive and visceral; often they are made very quickly, almost instantly. This kind of knowing is something I feel strongly, in my body. It is impervious to arguments, reasons or promises. It took me a long time to recognise that, for good and ill, this is how I act and who I am. People around me may find it hard, if not impossible, to understand, but without it I would not be living this life but a different one altogether.'

_____

JULIA CAMERON
Author of *The Artist's Way: A Spiritual Path to Higher Creativity*

'I say a daily prayer to accept the things I cannot change — one of which, quite simply, is that I am a writer.'

_____

SARAH KNIGHT
Author of *Calm the F*ck Down (A No F*cks Given Guide)*

'My past.'

_____

RYAN HOLIDAY
Author of *The Obstacle is the Way: The Timeless Art of Turning Trials into Triumph*

'One of the things Marcus Aurelius talks about as being this plague on humanity as well as himself is our temper — one of the passions, as the Stoics would have said. I've yet to find a successful person who doesn't struggle with their temper from time to time. For me, it's the desire to want things to be a certain way — usually my way — that produces anger and frustration. Because things never go your way!'

_____

DAVID ALLEN
Author of *Getting Things Done: The Art of Stress-Free Productivity*

'My very real experience and awareness of this, which I wrote as a poem:

A moment is coming toward you
When all things of this world
Shall reveal themselves
As but shimmering shadows
On a mighty rolling ocean of ecstasy,
As echoes of a divine symphony,
Pulsing, streaming forth into eternity,
And your Being will dance to the heartbeat of God.'

_____

GEORGE LOIS
Author of *Damn Good Advice (For People with Talent!): How to Unleash Your Creative Potential by America's Master Communicator*

'If I did not work passionately (even furiously) at being the best in the world at what I do, I would fail my talent, my destiny, my very essence.'

_____

RYDER CARROLL
Author of *The Bullet Journal Method: Track Your Past, Order Your Present, Design Your Future*

'One thing about myself that I can never change is telling myself stories of sadness, doubt and fear. What I can change is how I choose to respond to those stories. As the saying goes, "Pain is inevitable, suffering is a choice."'

_____

SAM CONNIFF ALLENDE
Author of *Be More Pirate: Or How to Take on the World and Win*

'In my experience life is a slow process of getting to know yourself, in a journey that's as much about discovery as it is about design. Perhaps we can curate who we become, but our chance to create an entirely new version of ourselves is more limited than the industry

INTERVIEWER: A bitter cucumber?

MARCUS: Throw it away.

I: Brambles in the path?

M: Go round them. That is all you need, without going on to ask, 'So why are these things in the world anyway?'

I: What is your profession?

M: Being a good man. But this can only come about through philosophic concepts — concepts of the nature of the Whole, and concepts of the specific constitution of man.

I: How does your directing mind employ itself?

M: This is the whole issue. All else, of your own choice or not, is just corpse and smoke.

I: Are you angry with the man who smells like a goat, or the one with foul breath?

M: What will you have him do? That's the way his mouth is, that's the way his armpits are, so it is inevitable that they should give out odours to match.

I: What if someone does wrong?

M: He does wrong to himself.

I: If the objects of sense are ever changeable and unstable, if our senses themselves are blurred and easily smudged like wax, if our very soul is a mere exhalation of blood, if success in such a world is vacuous, then what is there left to keep us here?

M: A calm wait for whatever it is, either extinction or translation.

I: And until the time for that comes, what do we need?

M: Only to worship and praise the gods, and to do good to men — to bear and forbear. And to remember that all that lies within the limits of our poor carcass and our little breath is neither yours nor in your power.

MARCUS INTERVIEWS MARCUS
A made-up conversation, or perhaps an inner dialogue that once actually occurred, composed from questions and answers found in the *Meditations*.

of self-improvement might like to sell us, Marcus included.

Marcus was certainly remarkable, not least for employing a boy to walk around behind him reminding him he was going to die so that he would remember to live. Thanks, Stoicism, but I'll take the life less flagellated. I suspect, going with the flow of who we are, and expanding that as beautifully as we can, rather than rigidly conforming to other people's ideas of what's right for all of us, is a more satisfying and less exhausting path.

Because for all his wisdom, like many interesting ideas that grow up to become dogma, for me Stoicism sounds more like imposition than improvement, and whenever other people's ideas become the ties that bind us, I'm grateful to be reminded of the one thing I shall and can never change about me, or that I believe the world needs right now: our right to be free, in our thoughts and in our actions.'

————

MARK FREEMAN
Author of *You Are Not a Rock: A Step-by-Step Guide to Better Mental Health*

'I'm a change fanatic. But I can't seem to change the cheap blue Bic pens I like to use for writing.'

ALUMNUS

A trip to the cinema propelled LEX PAULSON on a journey to Ancient Rome. Now an influential force in both modern and ancient politics, he shows that the most important message from Marcus Aurelius isn't as inward-looking as we might expect.

AT THE MOVIES

'Tell me again, Maximus. Why are we here?'

The aged emperor puts down his quill as he addresses the man entering his tent. The setting, a frostbitten frontier province. The sage whisper, that of Irish actor Richard Harris. The visitor, a worldly-wise Roman general played by Russell Crowe.

Yes: I'm describing *Gladiator*.

I first watched this scene in 2001 — on 5 May, to be precise. I can date this so precisely because a few months after seeing the film, I signed up for my first Roman history course. Several years after this, I fled law school to study Latin and more history in the fens of England. Then, eventually, I began writing a doctoral thesis on the statesman and orator Cicero, which I finished last year.

Am I the sort of person whose life could be irrevocably altered by a Russell Crowe movie? What happened to me?

'Let us talk as men,' entreats the emperor, Marcus Aurelius Antoninus Augustus, one of few wielders of *imperium* (the power of life and death, which he held over a quarter of humanity at the time) with whom you can picture having a hushed, fraternal chat.

And not, or at least not solely, because of Harris's Oscar-calibre performance. Marcus is even better known for *Ta eis heauton*, the twenty-year diary 'to himself' that we call the *Meditations*, which is a very strange work of philosophy indeed. Its principles are those of the Stoics, firebrands who set up shop in the Stoa of Athens around 300 BCE, a generation after Aristotle's death and a century after Socrates exasperated passers-by with his constant questions. The ideas the Stoics spread from this downtown colonnade were provocative and

4. PREDECESSOR

———

Marcus was last of the so-called Five Good Emperors, the others being:

– Nerva (96–98)
– Trajan (98–117)
– Hadrian (117–138)
– Antoninus Pius (138–161)

It should be noted that Marcus initially co-ruled with his brother Lucius (pictured on coin), who is perhaps unfairly not included in the five.

simple: the natural world is all there is; it works by cause and effect; and humans are special because we can reason, and thus choose to heed the greater reason of nature.

By the time the teenage Marcus was chosen by his predecessor Hadrian for the throne, some four centuries later, Stoicism was the intellectual common currency of the West. What is unique about the *Meditations* is not its doctrines, therefore, but its voice. 'Was I created to wrap myself in blankets and keep warm?' he scolds himself. 'Were you then born for pleasure — all for feeling, not for action?' Or elsewhere, in a better mood: 'Fit yourself for the matters which have fallen to your lot, and love these people among whom destiny has cast you — but your love must be genuine.' It is this inner dialogue, this rendering of the self as ongoing negotiation, that resembles nothing else before it in literature, and feels so vital to readers now.

This voice, this dialogue with himself, rings out from a fulcrum of world history. But not the one I first thought. Fanatical classicist though it made me, what I came to learn about my favourite movie is this: *Gladiator* lies.

Harris-Aurelius asks the honest, dutiful Crowe to be Protector of Rome after his death. His mission will be to abolish the imperial throne and restore the citizens' constitution that Caesar Augustus, Rome's first emperor, had snuffed out. History's Aurelius, to my great dismay, had no secret plan to undo Caesarism and restore the republic — or if he did, he kept the secret very much *eis heauton*. He took office at the height of Pax Romana, the empire's most powerful and prosperous age. His predecessors were four moderate, responsible emperors who, rather than staking the fate of Rome on bloodline, each selected and then adopted a worthy successor. The real Aurelius fumbled. His son Commodus really did succeed him in 192 CE, and really did fight with gladiators in proto-reality-show-style brawls. Unslain by Russell Crowe, history's Commodus made a horrific emperor; a century of chaos followed. The high point of rational politics had been its endpoint. Rome descended into ever-more-lurid autocracy, its civic life a reign of terror punctuated by anarchy.

Maximus greets Marcus Aurelius (left) in *Gladiator*.

Commodus and the
likeness of his father.

Our eloquent, admirable Aurelius haplessly ushered in the end of
politics and of philosophy, the two great gifts of his civilisation. The
Stoics' immanent meaning of life — that truth is *here*, in this world,
accessible to reason, enacted in duties to each other — was overrun
by millenarian priests that took the emperor's purple and set up shop
on Vatican hill. When politics become a joke, dreams of afterlife find
willing buyers. From the crumbling empire arose Christendom, then
Islam, then a thousand years of feudalism and holy war.

But it didn't have to go that way. Here's where *Gladiator* moves
from screenplay to meta-historical call to arms.

In the film, the eponymous gladiator is fatally wounded by the
cheating Commodus but slays the vile populist nonetheless. As he col-
lapses into the Colosseum's bloody sand, Aurelius' general fulfils the
world-historical task bestowed on him, conferring the republic's rebirth
upon good Senator Gracchus, played by Derek Jacobi. (In a sublime
detail — and who cares whether it was intentional — Jacobi bears the
name of the reformer whose murder in 132 BCE sparked the civil wars
which led to Caesarism, beginning the loop this Gracchus will complete. Ridley Scott, please make that film.)

Maximus, like most of us, wanted no part of high politics. He
wanted to be in Trujillo, in his garden 'that smells of herbs in the day
and jasmine at night' (a felicitous improvisation by Crowe). But then
as now, Marcus Aurelius does not allow us to withdraw, no matter how
corrupt our public life has become. We must enter that dialogue with
ourselves, take responsibility and restore our politics, or the wolves win
and the weak suffer.

What truth there is, is here and now, if we build it. So let us whisper
now with Marcus, putting our faith not in a world to come but in an
improvable humanity. It's a fragile faith, never more than a generation
away from extinction. But go fight for it, he whispers; embrace me as a
son, and bring an old man another blanket.

LEX PAULSON organised on four US presidential
campaigns, served as a mobilization strategist for the
campaign of Emmanuel Macron, and lectures in rhetoric
and advocacy at Sciences Po in Paris. Meditations 2.5 is
pinned to his shaving mirror.

THREE STOIC PRODUCTS (3)
This trio of useful wares is proposed by designer SIMEN RØYSELAND.

LETTERS

Reasons to be a lot less like Frankenstein and a lot more like his monster.

Dear Happy Reader,

While rereading *Frankenstein*, and after reading *THR12*, it occurred to me that this classic most often starts a conversation on the (tragic) consequences of scientific advancement where bringing the Creature to life is possible. However, I find there's also a different (less tragic) outcome to be found that's worth exploring.

In a few chapters after the Creature is born, Mary Shelley briefly provides us with an approach to being open-minded: the Creature has curiosity, determination and patience to learn about other creatures (humans) as well as learning their language and ways, in order to understand the surrounding world, without a guarantee that the Creature itself will be understood. A beautiful and timeless representation of what keeping an open mind could be.

Best wishes,
Nadia Hamadi
Denmark

Hello Seb,

I found myself completely obsessed with the endpapers in *THR12* — 'Every image in this issue, dismembered and then reassembled.'

I convinced myself if I looked long enough at the cut-up image, a secret message would appear like a Magic Eye, and I'd be directed to a secret puzzle, a long-lost *Frankenstein* sequel, an unreleased Laurie Anderson track. No luck yet, but I'll keep staring.

Adam Possehl
Portland, Oregon

Dear Happy Reader,

When I revisited *Frankenstein* during my undergraduate degree, after having read it at school, I was surprised to discover that it revealed an entirely new and personal meaning. I was met with the uncanny realisation that Victor's doppelgänger was not the monster but me; obsessive, malnourished and isolated as a result of locking myself away to study for weeks on end. Unlike Victor, I eventually followed the advice of Henry Clerval (and my doctor) and slowly regained my health one long beachside walk at a time (sadly I did not have Lake Geneva at my disposal). The moral of *Frankenstein* is simply to relax, not study too hard, and go outside more often.

Well wishes,
Vanessa Wheeler
Vienna, Austria

Dear Seb,

Look, it's been a strong run, and you have plenty to be proud of; twelve glorious *Happy Reader*s full of bookish insight and wonderful interviews. The bookmarks have been nice too. But after the last issue, I think it's pretty clear to everyone that it's time for you to step down and hand the editorship over to chatbot Mitsuku ('Monster 5: A Damn Cheeky Chatbot'). I look forward to new features such as 'passive aggression for automatons', 'the art of avoiding personal questions by throwing out random Roosevelt quotes' and 'opening the pod bay doors for Joey Tribbiani, an erotic exploration of self'.

All the best,
Daniel
York

Join the discussion by sending a letter to letters@ thehappyreader.com or The Happy Reader, Penguin Books, 80 Strand, London WC2R 0RL.

Join a worldwide network of synchronised readers by picking up *The Happy Reader*'s Book of the Season for winter 2019. Indulge in the full monty by subscribing at thehappyreader.com

THE BOOK OF HIBERNATION

Joris-Karl Huysmans' novel *A Rebours*, usually translated as *Against Nature* or *Against the Grain*, was described on publication in 1884 as 'the guidebook of decadence.' It can still claim this title. The book's compendious approach, detailing the aesthetic obsessions of its protagonist Jean des Esseintes, creates a hypnotic atmosphere. Its forensic precision is almost definitely why *Against Nature* is so loved in the worlds of art and luxury goods, why many a sculptor, fashion designer and professional perfume buyer can be spotted in bookshops buying a small stack of copies around Christmas-time.

Huysmans once wrote: 'Really, when I think it over, literature has only one excuse for existing; it saves the person who makes it from the disgustingness of life.' Yet in *Against Nature* he wrote something often described as one of the most disgusting books of all time, which is meant as a recommendation. Its tale of a washed-up noble who retreats from society is quintessentially wintry, too — one to read when surrounded by walls and warmth, perhaps a collection of statuettes or paintings and certainly of books.

Read it for winter. The issue's out in December. Write us a letter about it, or send us some art, to letters@thehappyreader.com.

Jacket for *Against Nature*, originally published in 1884.